**DATE DUE**

| | | |
|---|---|---|
| NO 14 75 | JA 7 94 | |
| MY 14 76 | MR 8 96 | |
| | HF 17 96 | |
| DE 2 77 | OC 31 00 | |
| JY 20 84 | | |
| MR 15 '85 | | |
| JE 16 87 | | |
| | | |
| OC 28 '93 | | |
| NO 19 93 | | |

# AFTER THE FIRST DEATH

# AFTER
# THE FIRST
# DEATH

A NOVEL BY DONALD TAYLOR

GEORGE BRAZILLER · New York

Standard Book Number: 0-8076-0675-8
Library of Congress Catalog Card Number: 72-93479

First Printing
Printed in the United States of America

Designed by Ronald Farber

ACKNOWLEDGEMENT

The poem by Dylan Thomas—"A Refusal to Mourn the Death,
by Fire, of a Child in London"—is reprinted by permission of
New Directions Publishing Corporation, from *The Poems of
Dylan Thomas* © 1946.

FOR A. E. AND C., AND
FOR J. AND FOR D., IN
LOVE, FRIENDSHIP, AND
IN MEMORY.

Never until the mankind making
Bird beast and flower
Fathering and all humbling darkness
Tells with silence the last light breaking
And the still hour
Is come of the sea tumbling in harness

And I must enter again the round
Zion of the water bead
And the synagogue of the ear of corn
Shall I let pray the shadow of a sound
Or sow my salt seed
In the least valley of sackcloth to mourn

The majesty and burning of the child's death.
I shall not murder
The mankind of her going with a grave truth
Nor blaspheme down the stations of the breath
With any further
Elegy of innocence and youth.

Deep with the first dead lies London's daughter,
Robed in the long friends,
The grains beyond age, the dark veins of her mother,
Secret by the unmourning water
Of the riding Thames.
After the first death, there is no other.

DYLAN THOMAS

# AFTER THE FIRST DEATH

1

WE LEFT THE TRACKS AFTER
crossing the river and walked down the embankment to
the edge of the trees. As we got to the trees a freight
train came by and we turned and watched until it was
long out of sight. Emile said there was a grade about
two miles ahead where the trains would slow down
enough for us to catch one.

"We'll do that in the morning," he said.

We walked into the trees and then out to a small
clearing where we could see the river. The sun was
going down behind two low hills far beyond the other
side of the river and the river reflected the light and it
was brighter than it had been a few minutes ago when
we crossed the bridge. I wondered if it would be cold
again. I couldn't sleep in the cold.

Emile went to gather kindling and wood for a fire and I opened the two cans of beef stew I had bought in the town where we were thrown off the freight we had been on since Idaho, that was going all the way to Los Angeles.

Emile came back and made a fire. He dug a shallow hole and lined the bottom with small rocks and then built the fire over them. He said the rocks would stay warm for a long time and when the fire got low there would be enough heat left in the rocks to keep the coals from going out. He smiled as he spoke. He worked like an old man who has done the same job all his life and who has loved every minute of it. Sometimes he talked quietly to himself, too, his watery-blue eyes fixed on whatever it was he was doing and yet not seeming to be seeing anything at all. I had met Emile the night before when we were outside Caldwell, Idaho, and we had to wait until near morning before a train came that was going in the direction we were. It had been a long and cold wait. Emile had complained about trucks taking over the land; trains didn't come as they used to. Emile was fifty, fifty-five, but he looked much older. He was a small man, hunched over. He had been the first one to tell me what the name Los Angeles meant. For some reason I always thought it had meant lost angels.

By the time we were through eating, the sun was down and the fire threw flickering shadows, slowly darkening, on the thick-trunked trees around us. It started to get cold. I got up and walked over to the river to wash my hands. The river was dark now, moving slowly. A short time ago it had been something different, something bright, cheerful, something that seemed to call you to run after it as it had been when I used to go fishing after school not long ago in Minnesota. It had been a narrow river then, too, and always bright in the late afternoon. But now it was dark, and there was something unpleasant about it, something mysterious as it slowly moved through the darkness; it was as though all I had associated with it before, and as I had remembered the river near home, was somehow false and that now, seeming to be a part of the darkness, it was as it was meant to be—cold and dark and silent. The sky was dark, too. Clouds had come up from the west and there was the smell of rain in the air. Toward morning I saw lightning, but it didn't rain.

I stayed there for a long time watching a small pool at the river's edge that had been formed by a fallen tree and where a fish was feeding. I tried to think of something I knew would soon begin to be important, but all the time I kept hearing the soft lapping of water and the occasional splash made by the fish feeding in the pool and I kept thinking how it would be to catch the fish and eat it; and after a while I went back to the clearing, shivering from the cold.

Emile was sitting by the fire, like an Indian with his legs crossed under him, a small but thick notebook open on one knee. He was writing something in it when I sat down. There was a long silence and I watched the shadows the fire threw on the trees around us. Emile wrote slowly, like a child, drawing each letter out carefully. I looked at the fire burning evenly between us

3

and at the shadow of Emile's body against the tree behind him. I moved closer to the fire but couldn't stop
shivering.

"What're you writing?" I asked.

He didn't answer at first, not until he had finished,
and then, looking very old from across the fire, he said
simply, "Just sort of a record of things."

I wanted to talk. It was good to talk because of the
cold. Emile looked at me, his eyes dancing from the
fire's light, and finally he said, "This your first time out?"

"Yes. At least this far."

"You really going to Los Angeles?"

"Yes," I lied.

"What about your folks?"

"What about them?"

He didn't answer for a while, and then he said, "It's
better country up north."

Emile went back to his notebook again and there was
only the sound of the fire burning between us and, at
times, a faint splashing from the river. He knew I had
lied to him when I had told him earlier where I was
going. I hadn't meant to lie to him but there was
nothing else I could say. I was going to Los Angeles but
only because it was warm there, because, before Emile
had told me what it meant, the name had always
fascinated me. I had lived there once as a child, there
and a lot of other places, and I remembered the beach
and throwing stones at the waves. Though it was hard to
remember more.

Emile put the book away and looked at the fire. And
then, as though speaking to himself, he said, "I met an

Armenian once. He used to say it was important that things be remembered. Crazy sort of a fellow. Always laughed when he spoke but all he ever talked about was how everything dies and is forgotten. He used to tell fortunes, too. He once told me he could tell when a man was going to die."

"How did he know that?"

"The eyes. You can always tell when a man's going to die by looking at his eyes. That's what he used to say. He told me if you look close at a man's eyes you can tell. He said there's something gray, like a film or something, that's over them, as though they don't really see what they're looking at."

I looked at Emile and tried to remember my father's eyes before he had died, what they had been like, what it was he had been looking at when he lay in the back of the trailer those last three days unable to say anything, just staring at the ceiling, the awful smell about his body. But it had all been too long ago.

"He used to keep a book, too. The Armenian. That's where I picked it up. It was full of all sorts of things. Names mostly. People he had met, tramps he had bummed with. Good towns, bad towns. Things like that. That's why he used to keep a book, so they'd be remembered, so they'd live a little while longer. Like I said, he was a crazy sort of fellow."

We said little after that. The fire burned down. Emile got up and put the last of the branches on it and then lay down beside it, his old khaki coat pulled up over his head. We didn't talk anymore and in a little while he was asleep. There was a sudden splash from the river as though something heavy had fallen into it, and from somewhere I remembered the last line from a poem about a child's death: "After the first death, there is no other." But I couldn't remember the rest of it or why I had thought of it at all and so I tried to think about keeping the cold away. Several times after that I hunted for more wood for the fire but it didn't help very much. Somewhere in the night the thought came to me that it might always be this way. Toward morning I became very cold. There was lightning, too, but it didn't rain.

2

EMILE AWOKE EARLY. I HAD MANAGED to keep the fire burning and I was putting more branches on it when he got up and stretched and then swore at the cold.

"You sleep all right?" he asked.

"Kind of off and on," I said.

"It's the goddamned cold," he said.

"Yes," I said.

Emile turned around and went behind a tree and pissed. When he came back to the fire he pulled two Hershey chocolate bars from his khaki coat pocket and gave one to me.

"It's always good to keep a little something for the next morning," he said.

I was hungry and the chocolate tasted good and I could smell the smoky wood-smell on my fingers when I put pieces of chocolate into my mouth. It reminded me of eating bacon.

I looked at Emile. I wondered what it would be like to live like that, to go from one dark place to another. He looked old and tired and his eyes were puffy and had something white like mucus in their corners.

After we finished eating we walked out of the clearing and up to the bridge. The river was bright again as the sun had just cleared the trees. I began to feel better, to feel warm. There were no clouds in the sky. It would be a good day.

We walked over to the embankment and then climbed it and began walking along the tracks. The grade was about two miles ahead and every once in a while Emile would turn and look down the tracks and listen. I listened, too, but I couldn't hear anything and I knew that Emile wasn't listening for anything, he was resting. We stopped and sat down just before we reached the top of the grade. Emile didn't look well. It took him a long time to get his breath and it seemed to hurt him when he breathed. But he didn't say anything, and his eyes looked better.

Emile explained how we were to catch the train. He said we were to keep out of sight of the engine and keep about two hundred yards apart. I was to wait there while he went farther ahead. If I could swing on all right I could then give him a hand; but if I missed the chance he would be able to see that I hadn't made it and we would both then wait for the next train. That way we'd be sure to stay together. It would be important to stay together, he said.

It was about two hours before we heard the train. I couldn't see it when it came but I could hear it far down the tracks. Emile had heard it first. He gave me a wave and walked up the grade. Emile was dirty and his clothes were things he had picked up from one place or another. He looked small and miserable as he walked away from me.

I went down the embankment and sat in the bushes. There still weren't any clouds in the sky. The sun was hot and mosquitoes were all around my face. I was nervous and hoped I wouldn't miss the rungs of the ladder of the car I was going to try for. The wheels were right underneath.

I still couldn't see the train but I could hear it now laboring up the hill. I felt the earth shake and could feel my heart beating faster. When the engine went by I stood up and climbed back up the embankment. I slipped on the gravel and had to scramble up on all fours. The train was moving faster than I thought it would be from the sound of the engine. I waited for a moment until I saw Emile climb up to the tracks from where he had been waiting. I waved to him and then began running. My hands were sweating and I didn't think I would be able to hold on to the steel ladder. The ladder was high up from the ground, the wheels turning right beside me. But then I saw I was running right along side an empty car whose door was wide open. Luck was with us. I ran faster and grabbed

9

the door frame and swung up into it with all my strength, and then gave a wild shout because I had made it. It was all over in a moment and I was inside the car on my knees. I turned around and looked out the doorway for Emile.

Emile was running, his hand outstretched. I reached out for him and our fingers almost touched and I could hear him breathing. I didn't think he was going to make it. He was pushing himself as hard as he could, his open coat flapping behind him, and I lay down on the floor of the boxcar and stretched my arm as far as I could. Emile was running hard and for a moment the space between our outstretched hands seemed too great, but then I caught his hand and pulled him into the car just as the train reached the top of the grade. He was old and he couldn't run anymore. It was why he wanted me to get on first, why we were to stay together.

Emile was breathing with difficulty, his chest rising and falling so that the top of his khaki coat nearly hid his face each time he gulped in air. His face was pale, nearly white in the faint light of the car. He sat leaning against the wall next to the door. The train picked up speed, shaking back and forth.

"Thanks, kid," he said. "I couldn't have made that one."

"Sure you could," I said.

He looked at me but didn't speak, his breathing making a sound I had not heard before, as though he had water in his throat, and then his head rolled to one side and he fell over as though he were an old doll suddenly pushed off a shelf. I didn't know what to do and was afraid to do anything and so I sat there and did nothing but look at him lying on the floor. After a long while I crawled over to him on my hands and knees and felt his wrist but couldn't find a pulse. I didn't like touching him, feeling his thin arm that was strangely heavy in my hand.

I was looking at his face when blood began to seep from the corner of his mouth and then from his nose. I had seen death before and I knew that when it came there wasn't anything anyone could do, and so I stayed there beside Emile and watched him and from the corner of my eye I could see the telegraph poles go by faster and faster.

Emile was a small man and wasn't very heavy. I moved him over to the open doorway of the car so I could see him clearly and then sat down against the opposite wall. He was framed in the doorway lying with his head on my coat. Beyond him there was blue sky and low brown hills and the sound of the train wheels clicking over the rails and I blinked my eyes each time the wheels went over the cracks where the rails were joined together. Emile looked as though he were sleeping, the light catching the thin gray hair of his head and the stubble of beard on his small face so that his head seemed to shine in the light. I was beginning to feel better because death had left and now I was alone in the car. I wondered what would have happened if I had let Emile go that moment when our fingers were only touching. He might have lived.

The train was going fast now when suddenly it lurched around a bend and Emile's body rolled over and then out the doorway. I crawled over to the door but the weeds were high and I couldn't see where his body had fallen.

Everything happened so quickly I hadn't realized I wet my pants; and that hadn't happened to me since childhood.

I moved away from the open doorway and sat back against the wall again. I couldn't understand the things that had happened. Everything seemed to be unreal. But I only thought of myself and my discomfort and that I was hungry. I didn't think of Emile until later when I remembered the book he had kept and wondered what would happen to it when they found his body.

3

THE TRAIN STOPPED. I SAT UP AND looked out the open door, trying to get my eyes used to the darkness. It looked as though we were in the middle of a desert. From up the track I could see two men walking alongside the cars looking at each one and trying the doors. They carried lanterns. The men stopped about six cars up to close a door and I took my coat and jumped down. My left foot turned under me when I hit the ground. I yelled and rolled over and down the small embankment and dropped my coat. The two men had heard me yell and they came running toward me. I didn't know what would happen if I got picked up. I managed to get to my feet and I started running into the night and away from the train. I heard the men call after me and I could see the beam of their lanterns dance on the ground around me. But they didn't follow me and their light didn't go far into the dark.

I kept running until I thought it was safe and then dropped to the ground behind a clump of bushes and waited. I could see the men looking into the boxcar I had been in and I could hear their voices but not what they said. They closed the door of the car. Then it was quiet. The men walked down the length of the train, their lanterns swinging back and forth, and I could hear them checking car doors as they went. I put my head down and waited. The earth beneath me was sand and full of small pebbles. I had been asleep in the car. I didn't know where the train had stopped or how long I had been asleep. My ankle hurt but I knew it would be all right and that it wasn't broken because I had run on it. But it did hurt. I hoped the men hadn't taken my coat.

The train started again and I looked up. There wasn't any question of trying to run for it. I watched it go, picking up speed easily over the flat land. I wondered if I was close to Los Angeles, if maybe this was it.

The train was long. There were one hundred and twenty-seven cars after the engine. It was nearly a record. I could remember only two or three longer trains. In Minnesota I used to watch the long freights come up from Chicago for the Twin Cities. One hundred and forty-one was the record.

There was a strange phosphorescence under the train as it pulled away, like a ship pulling out into a dark sea. When the train was gone I saw the lights of several buildings. There was a small town just on the other side of the tracks. In the quiet of the desert I could hear voices, and someone's laughter coming through the night, though it must have been a quarter of a mile away. I stood up and limped over toward the light. My coat was still where I had dropped it when I rolled down the embankment. I put it on and went up the embankment and sat on one of the rails to rest. I rubbed my ankle. It had started to swell.

The rails were already cold. I put my ear to one but couldn't hear anything at all. I couldn't see the light of the caboose either. It was as though the train had never been there. It had come out of the darkness and now it had gone back again. I didn't like where I was.

The town had maybe a dozen buildings. The closest one was a Shell gas station and I hobbled over to it and went into the men's room. It was dirty and there was a pair of coveralls hanging on a nail behind the door. I cleaned myself as best I could and combed my hair with my fingers. I felt better when I came out. There were three men working on an old Buick sedan in the garage of the station. They didn't pay any attention to me and I walked past them and out onto the street.

It was the only street I could see, a black strip laid down between dilapidated buildings. There was a tavern next to a dirt lot and between the gas station and a little alley that ran next to it. Half a dozen men were standing in front of the tavern on the sidewalk. Most of them held beer bottles in their hands. They were loud and I could see the one whose laughter I had heard from the other side of the tracks, a big man with a wide-brimmed hat pushed back on his head. Across the street from the tavern was a small cafe. There wasn't anybody in it, not even behind the counter. I went in and sat down. I was very hungry. I hadn't eaten anything since sunup and then only a chocolate bar. The clock behind the cash register said a quarter to eleven. I took the money out of my pocket and counted it again. I had seventeen dollars. One for each year.

I heard a toilet flush and a few minutes later an old man in a blue shirt came out wiping his hands on a white apron he wore around his waist. He told me the place was closed. He took off his apron and went back into the room he had come from. A moment later the outside lights went off. I went out and walked back to the gas station. Except for it and the bar, there wasn't anything else open.

I got some change for one of the dollar bills and tried the candy machine in the station office. But it didn't work. I told one of the men in the garage that the machine didn't work and that I had lost fifteen cents in it. He said to come back in the morning when the manager was there and he'd return it to me.

I didn't know what to do. I couldn't stand there and I didn't know where else to go. My ankle hurt very much now and I wanted to be where I could sit down, even for a little while. I couldn't go to the tavern because I was always questioned about my age.

I walked slowly up the street. Once past the tavern there wasn't anyone around at all. There was a small grocery store at the far end of the street where the street lamps ended. It was dark beyond that. I walked

16

around the grocery store. The back door was locked and so were the two windows I tried to open. I went back out to the road. I was in darkness now. The town was already behind me. I could see the headlights of a car about half a mile away cut across the road. I thought there must be a highway there. There was nothing else to do but to go to it.

I sat down by the side of the road a couple of times to rest. My ankle hurt badly and I thought that maybe I had broken something, or maybe cracked a bone.

The town behind me was like a ball of light. I couldn't hear the laughter anymore, though I could still see the men standing like dim shadows in front of the bar. I looked up at the sky. I had never seen so many stars. They were crowded upon one another as though there wasn't any more room in the sky. There was no moon. It was not as dark as it had appeared to be from the town. I could see a hundred or more yards in any direction. But I couldn't sit there for long. It was cold and it would be better to walk than sit by the side of the road. The ankle would hurt as much one way as the other.

It was a long time before I made the highway. The highway was divided and I didn't know which direction to take. I crossed one section of it and stood in the middle. There weren't any cars. I knew I hadn't made a very good beginning. I didn't want it to always be this way, the way it had always been. I wanted to find someplace light and warm. I didn't care where. I decided I would thumb the first car that came. It didn't matter which way it was going.

# 4

THE CARS DIDN'T COME. I LOOKED IN both directions, but there was nothing, no light, no movement, nothing but the silent stars touching the horizon. It was as though the sky had been on fire and these were the coals sparkling now that the flame had gone out. I sat down to rest my ankle and waited. Still nothing came. It was chilly but not yet cold. The ground was warm and I imagined it would be hot there during the day. I was beginning to feel sick to my stomach and I knew it was because I had eaten very little the last few days and nothing at all that day but a little chocolate; and I was dirty, I could smell the urine on my pants. I looked up at the sky, the stars glowing and filling the sky from one end of the world to the other, and then lay down. My mind began to wander. I couldn't control my thoughts, and it didn't matter if there were no cars; sooner or later I knew one would come. It didn't matter. I had nowhere to go. I would only have to wait and at some time a car would come. And it was pleasant to wait there, the stars overhead, the night like a blanket over me, the ground warm, my ankle throbbing to the beat of my heart but no longer hurting. It was pleasant, in its own way.

When I was little I used to sing "Somewhere, Over The Rainbow" when I was sent out to the pasture to bring the cows in for milking. The cows would have come in by themselves when the sun went down but it was one of the jobs I was given to do when I was little. The farm was very big and it was a long way from the barn to the north pasture by the woods where the cows always gathered to be in the cool shade of the trees next to the fence that closed off the woods from the pasture. The woods were very mysterious but the cows weren't afraid and they would stand there in the afternoons, their tails swishing from side to side to keep the flies away. It wasn't our farm but belonged to my grandfather and then to my uncle when grandfather died and we were there because we had no place else to go and didn't have any money. I had wanted to leave then, too, but couldn't because I was only eight or nine years old and Mother had said that there wasn't anywhere else to go. But there were times even then when it was very bad and I would wait until I was sure I was all alone and I would sing the song over and over again wishing I could be a bluebird flying over a rainbow or flying anywhere but where I was. There were times, too, when it was worse and my mother running into the bathroom with a butcher knife in her hands and locking the door behind her and me sleeping on the kitchen floor because the bathroom was next to the kitchen then and thinking I was in a sea of blood and years later seeing blood come out from beneath all the bathroom doors of wherever I was or whenever I would dream of that time which was often.

The stars were everywhere when I hid in the woods. I didn't bring the cows back that evening because I knew they would go home anyway once they were started and I kept on walking right across the pasture and to the woods at the edge of the farm which no one owned because it was very large and full of mystery and all the farmers used it for cutting timber and sometimes for hunting and I walked into the woods with the feeling I never wanted to come out again and the stars were everywhere and there was a small pool in the middle of the woods where once my uncle Ben showed me the prints of two deer in the soft dark earth around the pool and I remembered then too the lovely feeling of being next to the pool and not being afraid thinking that if the deer were still there even though it had been a long time ago that if the deer were still there they wouldn't be afraid of me because I wasn't afraid of them and I would sit there and watch them drink from the quiet water seeing the stars' reflection in the pool and then the soft rippling on the water as the deer drank and the stars dancing in the pool because of the ripples on the water and I remembered then the stories oh going back further and further sitting in a room on someone's lap being told about the twinkling stars and how they always watched over you each star given to each child born so that no one anywhere would ever be alone or unprotected there would always be a star there to watch out for you all the time and back further back to where there were no stars at all but only the soft wet warmth of dark sleep. . .

I sat up with a start. A heavy truck roared past, shaking the ground under me. For a moment I couldn't remember where I was. My head hurt. I didn't know how long I had been asleep. I tried to stand up but tried too quickly and when I got to my feet I couldn't keep my balance and I fell down. I thought very hard then that I would be all right and that I would just have to wait there on all fours and I would be all right. In a little while I did feel better and I got up slowly to my feet and just stood still breathing deeply the cool desert air, and then I walked over to the highway. The lights of a car shone far in the distance and I already had my hand raised so that when it approached the driver could see me.

But he didn't stop. Two more cars came by, one from either direction, but neither of them stopped. I had crossed the highway but didn't know which side would be the better, but as two of the cars had come from the side I was on I decided to stay where I was and to walk for a while. My ankle was sore but it didn't bother me. I was hungry and I didn't think of anything but wanting to find something to eat. I searched through my pockets as I walked to see if I had any gum or if there was anything I could eat. I found the cash register receipt for the beef stew I had bought two or three days ago, I couldn't remember when, and I put the paper in my mouth and chewed on it and then swallowed it. I didn't know if the scrub grass along the highway could be eaten or if it might make me feel worse and so I didn't eat any although I wanted to.

It was always the same dream though not always the same things happened. I didn't want to think about it. I thought about the headlights far in the distance. They were yellow and very bright and I thought they must be maybe two maybe even three miles away. I counted slowly until the car was close enough for me to raise my hand. It was traveling very fast.

As the car approached me it swerved over to the side of the highway and it seemed to be going too fast for the driver to stop for me. I had my hand up. It wasn't until the car was almost on top of me that I realized the driver had no intention of stopping at all. I jumped over to the shoulder of the road just as the car brushed past me, its right front wheel off the pavement and into the soft gravel of the shoulder, and then it swung sharply back onto the highway and drove off.

I had felt the car go past and it might have touched my coat but it hadn't hit me. I had kept to my feet and spun around as the car swept by me and back onto the road. All I could see was the blur of red lights. I didn't see what make it was or whether there was more than one person in it. I couldn't figure out why anybody would want to try to kill someone like that, to run someone down you didn't know or know anything about but to try to kill him anyway. I couldn't understand how anybody could do that. But I wouldn't forget the lesson.

It was a long time before another car came. I raised my hand and was careful not to be too close to the side of the road. The headlights came on slowly and I could see that the car was going to stop.


His name was Thomas Eckburton and he was a sales manager for an oil company. He asked me how far I was going and I told him just to the next all-night diner. I told him I hadn't eaten very much that day. He started driving again and asked me to lock my door. The car was new and smelled of newness and there were a lot of papers and ledger books and folders on the front seat between us. The dashboard lights were a soft green and I could see Eckburton's face in the windshield as he drove. He never took his eyes from the road at first and he talked all the time. He had a kind voice and a tired face and in ten minutes I knew a lot about him and his wife and his three children and his son who was having trouble in school and how he traveled up and down the length of California for his company.

"Then this is California?" I said.

He looked at me for the first time and repeated what I had said. I had meant it more as a statement than a question. But I wasn't sure. There weren't any signs the way I had come.

He looked at me again and asked if I had any money.

I told him I had enough. I just wanted to get something to eat.

He reached over and opened the glove compartment. The light was bright inside the compartment and there was a package of dried figs. I looked at Eckburton but he didn't take his eyes off the road.

"Help yourself," he said. Then, as an afterthought, "I'll have one, too."

The figs were sweet and I could feel the small seeds crush on my teeth and it felt good to swallow. I ate too fast and every once in a while I could see Eckburton look at me. He continued to talk but softly, almost as though to himself, but I wasn't listening to what he was saying. I thought of the figs and of how good they tasted. Then he cleared his throat and said, "Where're you from?"

I didn't answer him and he didn't seem to mind and we drove on for a while and then he asked again, "What's your name?"

There was always a brief feeling of panic whenever I felt myself being driven into a corner. I put the package of figs back into the glove compartment and closed the door and then it was dark inside the car again except for the soft green light from the dashboard. I remembered a small printed sign taped inside the glass top half of the door of the grocery store I had tried to break into. It said, In case of emergency, call Jason Canen. And then it gave an address and telephone number.

"Jason Canen," I said.

He turned on the car radio and soft dance music filled the silence between us. He kept his eyes on the road all the time and began talking again quietly, as though it made no difference whether anyone listened or not. He drove slowly and carefully and we could almost have been sitting still looking at the stars overhead. Only the ground was moving beneath us, swiftly, like a black current.

It was not a bad name. I thought afterwards as we drove through the quiet desert that it wasn't a bad name at all. Maybe it would make a difference.

5

RUTHIE'S A GOOD KID BUT SHE doesn't understand that to make a living in this world you have to do things which under other circumstances you wouldn't always do. All the traveling I do for the company, for example. I've got to do it or I'll never get ahead, never get anywhere. I'm home a good three nights a week, sometimes even four, but to listen to her you'd think I was never home. She means well, she's only concerned about the kids, and I can't blame her, but I get tired of it nonetheless. Another four or five years and I won't have to do all this driving. I'm tired and I'm getting afraid of having an accident. The company will give me a district office by then, and things will be better. The company's pretty good to its employees all in all.

Of course, she's concerned about Jimmy, and so am I, but what can I do? He's no older than you are and he's been arrested twice already for drinking under age. Of course, it really isn't drinking he's been doing, it's only been beer and that isn't anything like hard liquor. Hard liquor is drinking. There is quite a difference between beer and hard liquor. But it's got us all worried sick. Jimmy wouldn't use hard liquor. I know that. He's a good kid. I get to thinking that maybe there isn't anything anyone can do about it, I mean about drinking and what kids have to go through to grow up, that maybe it's just something we'll have to go through like in the last decade we had to go through the Second World War. This decade has its own problems, too, and we're just going to have to live with them until everything's been worked out. You're not old enough to remember the problems we had in the thirties but it was a hell of a lot worse then I tell you. I think we'll come out of it okay because we're all made of pretty good stuff when you come right down to it. People are pretty good. It's only a few who cause all the trouble. Jimmy's been a problem but he'll grow out of it. He's had to run with a pretty rough crowd in that damn high school he goes to. That's where the trouble is, right in the school. They don't give it the right attention. The problem. They go about it the wrong way. We're thinking of sending Cathy and Julie to another high school next year, when they're old enough. They're good girls and I don't want them spoiled by the rough crowd Jimmy's had to run with. Of course, it's different for a boy. There's a lot of rough things in life and you have to learn how to handle yourself. That's what I said to the probation officer, that it wasn't Jimmy's fault doing what he did, it was all part of what he had to do to stay with the crowd. You know what I mean. It's gotten to be some sort of tribal custom now. Everybody's got to do the same thing. Ruthie doesn't understand these things. Oh she knows in her own way but she doesn't really understand what a man has to go through to keep ahead these days. I was trying to explain this to her a couple of nights ago in the kitchen but she kept saying that well everybody has to do the same thing. And I suppose she's right but she still doesn't know what it really means. Not the way I do. I'm right in the middle of it all the time and I know how it feels. I'm tired and I know it. I'm forty-nine and I've been working all my life. In another four months I'll be fifty and half a century will have gone by. All the things that have changed in my lifetime: the car, the airplane, the atomic bomb, practically everything we know. I tried to explain some of this to the kids and the girls understood right away but all Jimmy could do was shrug his shoulders as though the automobile and the airplane and the atomic bomb weren't important to our lives. Of course, he's a good kid and he'll come out of it okay. Things are more complicated today and he's got more to learn than I had to. But he's had all the advantages, too. We've got a big home, lots of lawn, two cars; the kids even have their own television set. They've had all the advantages. I've had to work hard for these things; all this driving I do up and down California, for example, is all for them. Well, in four or five years all this will be over and we'll be able to settle down to a more nine-to-five routine and that'll make Ruthie happy. There's a diner up ahead. I'd stop with you but I'm going to try to make home tonight so I'm going to keep on going. I'll just let you off. I know the place. The food's pretty good. A lot of truckers stop there so you can always tell. You sure you got enough money? You looked kind of, well, you know, I wasn't too certain when you first got into the car. I don't usually pick up hitchhikers. It's against the company's rules. But I thought it wouldn't hurt just this once.

# 6

ECKBURTON WAS TALKING SOFTLY, HIS hands on the wheel, his eyes, looking through the reflection of his own face, staring down the road. He was a kind man and I wanted to thank him for helping, for picking me up and for giving me the figs and for not asking too many questions. I was thankful for that. He talked all the time, and it didn't seem to matter whether I was listening to him or not. He talked quietly and I thought that he probably talked in just the same voice when he was alone, too, when he was alone in his car driving up and down the length of California for the company that would take good care of him.

I looked at the night, at the flat land touched with stars. I could see my own reflection in the side window.

It was like looking at a ghost, a shadow riding on the other side of the window floating swiftly through the desert night watching me watching it. I was fascinated by the shadow, the shadow of myself floating silently beyond the window, turning as I turned, looking as I looked. I closed my eyes and he did not go away, he had only closed his eyes, too, and we were back together again, back where we had always been, and he was saying to me that I had to get away, that I had to find what there was to find of my life before something happened and it would then be too late because so much had already happened. Pieces scattered to so many places that I didn't know anymore whether they would ever come together again.

I had dropped out of school that spring, and one day in the early afternoon I walked down to the railroad tracks not far from where we lived and there was a freight train sitting there as though it were waiting for me. I had never ridden a freight train before, though I had often watched them. Sitting up on the hill I had watched the long trains come up from Chicago. But this one was headed in the other direction, and it was just sitting there, the engine far ahead enveloped in a cloud of white steam. When I got to the train I climbed aboard an empty boxcar and sat in the open doorway not thinking about anything, and after a while the train began to move and I watched the tall grass slowly slip away and the telegraph poles like witnesses to a funeral pass silently before me, and I let myself be carried away. No one was there to ask me why. No one was there to see. As the train picked up speed, but never traveling fast, it passed little towns and stations, and occasionally groups of children and once an old man turned to look at me sitting in the open doorway with my legs hanging out of the door, and they waved to me and I waved back to them and it was as though it was my farewell, their hands raised long into the distance, my hand waving back.

I had not thought it would be that way, I had not thought I would leave so suddenly, without a word, a letter, left behind. But I did, and that was the beginning, or the end, or both, the end of one time and the beginning of another.

# 7

IT WAS APRIL THEN AND THE NIGHTS were cold. Home had always been motion, the moving from one place to another, so that motion itself became, after a while, the only permanent thing. But it was never traveling. It was escape, the leaving of one bad experience after another. And there was never enough to eat. It was the one thing that made everyplace the same. That and the cold.

Sitting in Eckburton's car I remembered the tightness in my stomach, and watching the highway move silently beneath us it was as though nothing had changed. I had only moved from the back seat up to the front.

"Where are we going this time," I had asked.

"Florida," said my father.

"Where's Florida?"

"Down by the ocean. You'll like it there."

"Will it be warm?"

"Yes," he said. "It'll be warm."

"That's good because I'm cold."

"Wrap the blanket around you and your sister," said my mother who always rode next to my father in the front seat of the old Pontiac. "Try to sleep."

"How long can we stay?" I asked.

"Where?" said my father.

"In Florida," I said.

"Hush," said my mother.

And my sister Ann, who was older than I was, sitting in silence, staring out of the side window.


The aluminum sides of the diner rippled the lights of Eckburton's car as we drove into the driveway. Large squares of yellow light fell on the gravel. There were four cars and two large trucks parked in front of the diner. I thanked Eckburton as I got out of the car and watched him as he drove away, carefully stopping for the bump of the driveway where it rejoined the road; and then he was gone, his red taillights slowly disappearing down the highway toward home.

I went into the diner and sat down at the linoleum counter. Country music was playing on the jukebox and for a while no one paid any attention to me. Then an old woman with bluish-gray hair came from the kitchen and brought me a glass of water.

I ordered the first thing that came into my head, two

eggs with ham and toast. I couldn't think of anything else. I asked for a large glass of milk and if I could have it right away while the order was being cooked. She wrote everything down in a neat script on a green pad and then left without saying a word and returned to the kitchen. When she came out she carried a large glass of milk and it had bubbles on top of it like those in the pail under a cow that was being milked. I drank the milk down without lowering the glass and the waitress stood there watching me all the while. I told her thank you and asked her for another glass and wiped my mouth across the back of my hand. There was a worried look on her face. She went to get the second glass of milk and I took some money from my pocket and put it on the counter. When she came back she gave me the second glass and looked at the money on the counter and then walked away looking at a man a little ways down the counter from me.

It was then that I was sick. It came up all of a sudden and I vomited over the counter and then on the floor between two stools. I was shivering and my face was wet with perspiration.

I sat there leaning on the counter, my face down toward the floor, one hand on the stool next to me to keep from falling, and I could hear the silence of the people in the diner as they watched me. The music had stopped and the last thing I remember was someone coming out of the kitchen saying "Jesus Christ!"

I came to in a booth by the windows. Only a few minutes had gone by. A man with his back to me was mopping the floor where I had been sick. The waitress stood at the end of the counter holding my order of ham and eggs on an oval platter. I told her thank you again and that I was sorry, I was very sorry, and put my face in my hands to rub my eyes. My hands shook and my face felt cold although I didn't feel like throwing up any more. The waitress brought the order to the booth and set it down on the other side of the table. She put a green piece of paper face down on the table. It had Thank You Call Again printed across the back. On top of it she placed three one dollar bills, two quarters and a dime. Then she went back to the counter and brought over the second glass of milk. I remembered that I had left a five dollar bill on the counter.

I waited a few minutes and then got up and went to the washroom. There was soap and warm water there and I took a long time washing my face and hands. I hadn't vomited on my clothing but I could still smell the dried urine on my pants. On the wall between the washbasin and the toilet someone had drawn an exaggerated penis with a naked woman sitting on it waving an American flag. From the diner I could hear music, the same country tune that had played earlier.

I went back to the booth and sat down and pulled the plate of food over to me. It was cold now and the eggs were a soft white and little circles of grease had already dried around the edges of the plate. I began to pick at it slowly. I wished I had ordered a sandwich so I could have taken it with me and there wouldn't be any waste.

I looked up and could see my father's blue face. We were sitting around a table in a little roadside restaurant next to a motel somewhere in Nebraska and my father's face turned blue. The food had just been brought to the table and Mother spoke to Father and he didn't answer but just sat there and then fell out of his chair and onto the floor. He always carried a small brown bottle of nitroglycerin pills in a trouser pocket and Mother hurriedly got it out and gave the bottle to me while she held his head, opening his mouth with her fingers.

"Put one in his mouth, quickly," she said.

The people in the restaurant were standing around me as I took the top off the little bottle and tried to get one small pill to come out. But the pills all came out in my hand and I didn't know what to do while Mother was telling me to hurry. I dropped them all on Father's chest and then picked one up and put it in his mouth. Mother was holding his head in both her hands and she told me to push the tablet back into his throat with my finger, and I did though it wouldn't go very far back because of his tongue.

Whether or not it was because of the pill I had pushed into his throat I don't know but Father did not die from that heart attack. There would be others to come just as there had been others before that I had not seen. But he did not die then and in a while the color came back to his face and we were able to carry him to the motel next to the restaurant. We were hungry that night because the attack had come before we had had a chance to eat, and the restaurant was closed by the time the doctor left. I remember Mother having to wire her sister for money to pay the motel bill. We had stayed there for a week waiting to see whether Father would die.

It was cold and there was nothing for my sister and me to do but to walk up and down the highway waiting for night to come. I watched the cars, wondering how they worked, how they were driven. I would go sit behind the wheel of our car, which had been parked by someone behind the restaurant, and I could barely see over the steering wheel. I tried to remember all the things Father did which made the car move and turn and stop, how the gearshift lever first went one way and then the other. Mother did not know how to drive. We ate sandwiches then, carefully dividing them to make them last.

8

I SAT IN THE CAFE FOR A LONG TIME
staring at the food in front of me and at the dark brown
back of the booth across the table, at the countless in-
itials and marks carved into it by the countless people
who had sat there as I did, eating food so they could
go on again to some place else. Milestones of a pointless
journey. On the train coming across the country, across
the flat rich land of middle America, a land full of
promise that was always somehow withheld, I hadn't
thought of where I was going almost as though it hadn't
been important, but only of where I had been for seventeen years—the trailers, the apartments, the moving from
one place to another. I knew the land, though only as
one who watches it pass beneath him, and I did not

like it. Money seemed to have the only importance and it tore you apart if you didn't have it. Into pieces scattered all over the land.

And the pieces never came together. They were scattered like autumn leaves over all the years that had gone before. Wherever I was I had been there before, had watched through the windows, through the muddied glass, the sights that now I saw. And they were always passing, and I was always there to see them go, to see myself go with them, leaving a part of me behind. I couldn't remember why I had left home that day, except that there had never been a reason to stay in a home that never was. It had almost been an accident getting on board the train, climbing into the empty boxcar, and how many days ago that had been I couldn't, or didn't want to, remember.

The train had taken me some place else, changing the scenery of what was around me, though the pictures I saw in my mind were the same as those I had always seen. Like wearing glasses too thick to see through, everything was turned inward and I became a constant spectator at the spectacle of myself, and my eyes ached.

I left the diner and went back out to the highway. I had drunk the milk, slowly this time, and had eaten one of the slices of toast with it. I had put the ham on the other slice of toast and had folded it over and wrapped it in a napkin and had taken it with me. I couldn't eat the eggs, though I had tried to eat them.

I walked past one of the two large diesel trucks and there was a man standing next to the cab. He had one foot up on the running board and he turned back and looked at me. He had been in the diner. He was short and blond and he wore a plaid shirt. He opened the door of the cab and then asked if I wanted a lift, his face hidden by the shadow of the truck.

"Get in on the other side if you want to come," he said.

He didn't wait for an answer but just got into the cab. I stood there for a moment and he started the engine. The noise was loud and I walked around the cab to the passenger side and climbed up and sat down next to him.

He didn't say anything and neither did I until we had cleared the driveway and were out onto the highway.

"My name's Whitaker. What's yours?" he said.

I thought for a moment, and then said, "Jason Canen."

"Are you feeling better?"

"I'm sorry I was sick back there. I couldn't help it."

"You don't need to be sorry. No one can help those things."

"I drank the milk too fast," I said. "I was hungry."

"I know. I was watching you."

He was still shifting the big truck to get it up to highway speed. I had driven a car before but I had never been in a diesel truck and I was confused by the levers he had to operate to get the truck moving. Each time he shifted the truck went a little faster.

"You looked as though you could use a lift," he said.

"Which way are we going?" I asked.

"South," he said, and then added, "The sun's almost up."

He wasn't surprised at my question, and I liked him

for that, for not saying more than was necessary. I looked past his silhouette at the eastern sky. The outline of the mountains was visible in the distance. The sky was still black but the stars did not seem as plentiful as before. Then slowly they went out one by one as I watched them, and the sky softened, and I could see the mountains more clearly. The black had given way to purple, then to gray, then to the soft young blue of morning.

We were traveling fast, the truck high off the ground. It seemed to cover the whole road and Whitaker handled it easily, his hands lightly on the wheel. I could see him a little better now. He had sandy-colored hair and a young face. He didn't look to be much older than I was. He had a bad scar down the right side of his face and over his ear. It looked like a birthmark, or a burn.

"Do you know where you're going?" he asked.

"No."

I was too tired to pretend or to lie or to want to be careful of what I said. I listened to the heavy sound of the powerful truck, the floor of the cab vibrating under my feet, and I could feel the weight of the trailer pulling behind us.

"What's in the truck?" I asked.

"Irrigation pumps, a generator; a lot of big machinery," he said.

There was always a trailer behind us. But not a large silver trailer pulled by a powerful truck. It was a small red trailer made out of plywood and it was always cold and damp and smelled of kerosine. We pulled it along after us wherever we went, slowly, the old Pontiac over-heating and stalling often. It was like a curse that followed behind us, and into which we entered each night to sleep. From city to city, trailer park to trailer park, a sick old man looking for work that was forever available in the next town, the next state, tomorrow.

"What're you going to do when you get there?"

But I didn't answer. I had closed my eyes and pretended I was asleep, and in my mind I could hear Mother saying to Father, "Hush, they're asleep now."

"Helen, I think it might be better if we went south."

"I'm so tired, Joe."

"I know. I am, too."

"I don't want to move again."

"We can't stay here."

"Why not?"

"What do we live on?"

"We'll manage, Joe."

"Borrowing from your sister?"

"She doesn't mind. She knows how it is."

"I don't want to stay."

"Joe."

"I've been everywhere, asked everybody, read all the papers. There isn't any work."

"Maybe I could find something."

"No, Helen, that won't do."

"Shhh . . . The children. Let's not wake them."

"Let's try south. Florida's warm. There's a lot of opportunity down there."

"But that's why we came west."

"I got sick. I didn't count on that."

"I know, Joe, I know."

"I think we can make it on what we have."

"But what are we going to do when we get there?"

"I don't know."

I looked up. Whitaker was looking at me. "I said, what are you going to do when you get there?"

I could feel the truck vibrating under me, the roar of its engine like a sound that seemed to carry us on it. I looked up and the sky was light, the blacktop road moving swiftly beneath us.

"Where're we going?" I asked.

"South. The Mexican border. You all right?"

"Yes," I said. "I'm all right."

"You were asleep."

"Was I?"

"Sorry I woke you."

I sat up in the seat and brushed my hair back and rubbed my face, my fingers underneath my glasses.

"I guess I'll work," I said.

"What?"

"I said I guess I'll find work down there."

We drove on for a long time without saying anything. Then Whitaker lifted his chin and said, "There's trouble up ahead."

I looked and could see three or four cars in the distance pulled off the highway. Two of them were police cars, their red dome lights revolving. Whitaker switched on the truck's outside lights and began blinking them as he slowed down.

I could see now that there were two more cars beyond the police cars. There were black skid marks across the

44

highway, from the left lane across over to the right, where a car had crossed over out of control. The two cars were both on their sides, one further away almost out into a field where it had rolled over.

We slowed down to nearly a walk while one of the state policemen waved us on. Whitaker rolled down his window and spoke to the policeman as we passed.

"Anyone hurt?"

"Yeah, but keep moving."

Whitaker began shifting the truck into higher gears as I looked down at the wrecked car in the field. It was new and there were papers and folders and ledger books scattered all around it.

## 9

I CLOSED MY EYES AND PRETENDED I hadn't seen the car. I closed my eyes and sat back in the seat and put my hands under my legs to control the shaking that had come over my body and I thought hard of what it would be like wherever it was I was going or where I had been or people I had known or even to count numbers as fast as I could in my head. I remembered the candy machine that hadn't worked and that I had lost fifteen cents in it the night before and that I was supposed to go back there this morning to see the manager. I tried to think of what was inside the machine, of my fifteen cents somewhere inside of it, of the wheels and levers and slides where the coins moved mysteriously in the darkness of the machine. I thought of everything I could think about and after a while I had shoved the car out of my mind except for the sound of Eckburton's voice which I heard now as though he were sitting next to me and I knew I would never be able to forget entirely.

After a while I could forget almost anything I wanted to by just keeping it far enough away, by turning it off in my mind so that it didn't exist any more. But there were always a few things I couldn't forget and death was the hardest one of all. Death was always in front of me or behind me or somewhere close to me so that wherever I went or whatever I saw death was there, too. And sometimes I couldn't help thinking that death was inside of me, that we were a part of one another. Everything died, everything that was tried or planned or hoped for died before it could get very far. Maybe that was the way it was supposed to be, maybe that was why I had left, to escape the death I had lived with for seventeen years. Except that it didn't do any good. I hadn't escaped it at all but had merely taken it with me. Maybe if I could find a room somewhere and go into it and close the door and board up all the windows and then just stay there in the room forever and ever there would no longer be any death because it would be with me and I wouldn't let it out. I would keep death with me just as it had always been with me.

The sun was high and it was hot in the cab though a soft wind blew through the open windows. I sat up, I hadn't remembered opening my window and knew then that I must have been asleep. We were in the parking lot of a shopping center in what looked like the outskirts of a small city. I didn't feel well. I was aware of the smell of my clothes in the warmth of the cab. Whitaker was looking at me and the scar on his face was ugly and I wanted to turn away from him when he opened the door of the cab and stepped down. He started to dig some clothes out from under the front seat and said he was going to wash them. He said he would wash mine too if I would take them off. He said I smelled pretty bad and he smiled when he said that and I forgot about the mark which covered nearly half of his face. I said all right and started to get undressed. I took off all my clothes and gave them to him out the window and he made a bundle on the ground out of one of the shirts he had. I watched him walk away over the blacktop and across the yellow lines of the parking lot to a laundromat about one hundred yards away. I thought of Emile, remembering how he had walked away from me up the tracks, and then how his body had rolled out of the boxcar. I was sorry I had stared at Whitaker's face.

I sat in the cab for a long time. It was quiet except for an occasional car or truck on the highway behind us, and it was very hot. The sun was overhead. It felt good to be warm, to sit quietly, and I wondered what Mexico would be like if I went there. My left ankle was blue all around the anklebone and there was a yellowish-green ring around the part that was blue and it hurt when I touched it. But it didn't bother me if I left it alone.

I was naked in the cab though I still had my dungaree coat. But it was too warm to put the coat on or to put it over my legs. I held the ham sandwich wrapped in the napkin and the money I had taken from my pockets when Whitaker went to wash the clothes. There was $15.45 left. It wasn't very much to go very far with. For a moment I was afraid that Whitaker wouldn't come back with my clothes. I wanted to get out and go back to the highway. I wanted to keep going on. It was better that way. To keep going. But the feeling passed after a while and I began to think that maybe Mexico was too far and that I should think of what would happen when the money was gone. I would have to do something.

There was never enough money, sometimes not even enough to buy food. At school, my sister and I used to ask other children if we could share their lunches because, we would say, we had forgotten ours. But it was never true and the other children soon learned that we seldom brought anything to eat and they used to avoid us when it was lunch time. And once one of our teachers sent a note home with my sister about our not bringing lunch to school, and we never went back after that. We moved again a week or two later. I don't remember where.

I looked over to the laundromat. There was a large food market next to it. The only time I was caught stealing was when I stole a package of cupcakes from a market. I ate the cupcakes on the way home from school and didn't know that the man at the market had followed me to the trailer park. He came to the door just after I came in and he told Mother what I had done. She didn't say anything at first. She looked at me and then at the man, and then she said she would pay for the cupcakes and that she would punish me for having taken them. She looked through her purse and in several drawers in the chest at the back of the trailer where there was a double bed where she and Father slept. The man waited outside, holding the screen door open. But there wasn't any money, not even enough to pay for the cupcakes, and the man, who had waited all that time without saying a word, said she could send it to the market, and then he turned around and left. I remember the sound of the screen door slamming shut after him and that flies had come into the trailer.

But she didn't punish me. She went into the kitchen area and began to clean the metal sink, slowly wiping everything two or three times, and wouldn't look at me or say anything but just continued wiping the sink and the counter top over and over again. I was seven then, or maybe eight.

I was staring at the market across the parking lot when I saw Whitaker come out of the laundromat and go into the market. After a few minutes he came out carrying a package and then went back to the laundromat. It was hot in the cab and I wished he would come soon so I could get dressed and could go on again.

The hills behind the town were brown and low and the sky was a bright blue. It was hard to look at the sky for very long at a time. There were no clouds. There were only a few cars in the parking lot. Nothing seemed to move, even the flies on the inside of the windshield were motionless, like pieces of dirt on the glass.

It was a long time before Whitaker came back. He had waited for the clothes to dry, he said, when he did return. He brought with him a wet towel and I wiped myself down with it and it felt very good as the warm air dried my body. Whitaker tied the wet towel to his outside mirror to dry. I got dressed again and Whitaker got into the truck leaving his door open and opened the bag he had brought with him. There were two sandwiches in it and two bottles of orange soda and some cookies. I had put my money back into my pocket and I thought that I should pay him for my share. But I didn't mention it.

Whitaker's first name was Tenley and he didn't like it and said no one had called him anything but by his last name. He was from Kentucky and had come west three and a half years ago. He was shy and he spoke quietly in a soft voice, his words often running together. It was hard not to stare at his face. I found it fascinating and looked at him whenever I could and when I thought he wouldn't notice. I wondered what it would be like to go through life marked as he was. The birthmark was deep purple and began at his forehead and covered the whole right side of his face including his nose and upper lip and part of his lower lip and chin. His eyes were light blue and they seldom rested on any one thing for very long as though he were embarrassed or ashamed to be caught looking at anything. He had waited outside the cab until I had dressed, walking around the truck checking the tires.

We ate lunch in the cab leaving both doors wide open to catch whatever breeze there was, and when we were through he asked me if I wanted to ride down to Imperial Valley where he had to deliver the truck. He had been hired for only the one trip. He didn't have a regular trucker's license and only drove when there was a shortage of regular drivers. The shippers had given him papers saying that a license had been applied for, in case he should ever be stopped, and that was always good for one trip. But he'd have to turn the papers in with the truck. The union only wanted a certain number of regular drivers.

"But I don't care about it," he said. "I figure it's been good enough so far. There's probably another rig to take back up. Lettuce, or some kind of truck crop, and a new set of papers. If not, I can always do something else for a while."

"What's it like in Mexico?" I said.

"Hot, and no work. Or so I've heard. I've never been there. They use a lot of Mexicans in the Valley. Is that where you're heading?"

"I don't know," I said.

"I wouldn't want to try it myself," he said. "I've heard it's a pretty rough deal down there. They don't much like Americans, and I can't say I blame them. You should see how the Mexican workers are treated in the Valley. Makes you sick sometimes."

He stopped as though uncertain of what to say next, and then he said, "You do something?"

"Where?"

"Where you come from."

"No, I haven't done anything," I said.

"Sorry; don't mean to poke into what's none of my business."

"It's all right," I said.

"Where're you from?"

"Minnesota."

"Christ, that's a ways off. When d'you leave?"

"Maybe a week ago. It's kind of hard to remember," I said.

We sat there for a while and I tried to think of what I should do. Whitaker reached out and swung his door shut. I left mine open. Then he looked at me, the light hitting him full in the face.

"You coming?"

I didn't answer him.

"You're welcome to," he said.

I waited for a moment, looking at his face, and then away at the market across the parking lot.

"No," I said, turning back to him. "I guess not."

He looked surprised, and for a second I was sorry I had said that. But I got out of the cab and stepped down to the blacktop. I felt the soreness in my ankle.

"Thanks for everything," I said.

"Don't mention it," he said; and then, quietly, "Good luck."

I shut the door and stepped back. I waved at him as he started the diesel. He pulled the truck around in a big circle in the empty lot and stopped next to me.

"You sure you don't want to come?"

I could barely hear him over the sound of the engine noise. From this side of the cab, I couldn't see the birthmark. I raised my hand again and then let it fall. I shook my head. It was better not to begin. I didn't want to begin anything until I had found something left from all that had gone before.

10

I STOOD AND WATCHED AS THE LARGE
trailer-truck maneuvered out of the parking lot and then
went back onto the highway. The truck seemed to
hesitate for a moment, and then it slowly picked up
speed and drove off, the white towel flapping in the
wind. In a few minutes it was gone. Another truck came
by from the other direction and I remembered what
Emile had said about trucks taking over the land. I
thought then of Emile and of the book he had kept and
I wondered what must have happened to it. For a
moment I was sorry I hadn't gone with Whitaker. I had
been attracted to him, and his ugliness fascinated me.
But I didn't want to begin anything again. I wanted to
be by myself and see if I could find out why it was that

everything fell apart. I was beginning to understand, too, what I was doing, that I wanted to go to some of the places where I had lived earlier as a child and to see if I could find some of the pieces of myself that had been left behind. I couldn't go on until I had gone back, back to where it had all begun. Maybe then I could make some kind of sense out of what had been my life up until now. Maybe the thought of death would leave me then, too, and maybe then when I had found all the pieces I could start all over again.

There was a gas station across the highway and I went to it and asked for a map of California. I opened it in the office and stared at the blue and red lines criss-crossing themselves over the page and realized I didn't know where I was. I asked the attendant in the office and he pointed to where we were on the map. Then he left the office and went into the garage next door. There was another man in the office who remained. He was fat and he sat on the window ledge smoking a cigarette.

"Hot as hell out there, isn't it?" he said.

A dog came in from the garage and went first to the fat man and then to me. I had put my coat down on a chair next to the counter and the dog began sniffing at the coat. The ham sandwich was in one of the pockets. I picked up the coat and the dog sat down, its head cocked to one side, its tail wagging across the tile floor.

I spread out the map on the counter and tried to measure how far I was from the coast. It seemed like ninety or a hundred miles. It had been a long time since I had seen the ocean. My family had gone to California when the war broke out, Father saying that work could be found there, and we had lived in trailer parks in four different cities all around Los Angeles.

I thought of Carl then. We had been friends when I had lived near the ocean five or six years before. I was twelve then and small and nearsighted. It had been discovered only that year that my eyes were weak and that I had to have glasses. The school I went to then paid for the glasses because we couldn't afford them. My sister Ann had dropped out of school about that time.

"It's too hot to travel," the fat man said. He still sat smoking a cigarette. He had yellow fingers where he held the cigarette and yellow teeth and he hadn't shaved. "Hot as hell out there," he said again.

I was twelve then and for seven months we lived in a trailer park not far from the ocean. Carl and I used to walk on the beach together after school and throw stones at birds. Once one of us hit a gull and we were both sorry because the other gulls came and started to attack the one we had wounded. We drove the other birds away with more stones and went to the bird we had hit and stayed with it until it had recovered enough to fly off by itself. We threw stones at the waves after that.

I wanted to go and find Carl and see if maybe we could walk along the beach again. Maybe we could just talk about the time I had lived not far away and I could tell him about all the places I had moved to since that time and how we finally had to leave California because of Father's heart. He had found a job in a defense plant just before he had had his first heart attack. It was funny in a way, everything was going to be all right, and for a few weeks we had even moved out of the trailer into an apartment. Then it fell apart again, as it always had. But I wanted to find Carl.

I took with me a handful of book matches from the box next to the cash register and left the station office and went around the side to the men's room. When I came out the fat man was standing in the sun smiling at me. He asked me if I wanted a ride and I told him no and walked back out to the highway and then along the highway until I couldn't see the station any more.


It took most of that afternoon to reach the coast. I had gotten several rides but none of them took me very far, and one ride let me out on the side of the highway and then turned down a dirt road and it took nearly two hours before I was picked up again, and then for only a little ways.

I saw the ocean at sundown. An elderly man and woman had given me a ride in the back of their truck and they had let me out on the Pacific Coast Highway just before they turned south. When I got out of their pickup the ocean was in front of me, the sun going down behind it. I ran across the highway and then all the way across the beach in the soft sand until I came to what seemed like the beginning of the world. I forgot everything that had happened during the last few days, of where I had been or what I had done, and for a long time I just stood looking at the ocean with the waves rolling in to where they nearly touched my feet. Maybe it would work, I thought. I picked up a stone and threw it far into the waves.

## 11

I WALKED ALONG THE BEACH THINKING of Carl, that he could help put one more piece of the puzzle back into place. The sun was now down and the ocean had turned gray. There was no longer any line on the horizon between the earth and the sky and the sky itself seemed to be lifted out of the ocean. Waves of clouds rolled overhead, dark and distant.

I walked along the water's edge until it was dark and then went back to the highway. I remembered where Carl lived for I had often been there, had often eaten in the restaurant his parents owned and over which they all had lived. It was on the beach somewhere between Ocean Park and Santa Monica.

But everything had changed so much I couldn't recognize anything that I might have known before. I got a ride with a man who drove very cautiously through the heavy traffic and I watched for signs along the way that might tell me something of where the restaurant was. I asked the man if he knew of a restaurant owned by a family named Rigetti. He said he didn't.

I had not remembered the highway being built up with stores and apartment buildings along its sides. The beach had once been visible from the highway where now it was blocked from sight for miles at a time. But a few things were beginning to become familiar. We were in Santa Monica when I asked the man to let me out.

I began walking back toward the way we had come. A few things were the same, but not as I had remembered them from years ago. I walked past the restaurant itself before I realized it was there, that it was what I had been looking for. It seemed smaller now, somewhat run-down, and there were buildings on either side of it where once it had stood by itself on the beach with only a small garage next to it. Carl had been building a surfboard in the garage. What looked like apartment buildings were now on either side of it. The restaurant had had a back dining room that looked out onto the beach. I wondered if it was still there. I couldn't see the beach from where I stood.

The restaurant was full of people. I could see Carl's mother talking with a man by the cash register. Her hair was gray now and she looked heavier. The apartment above the restaurant was dark. I went around the side to where the wooden stairs led to the apartment and went up them slowly. I stood before the door for a few minutes before I knocked on it, and then softly, almost afraid of what might come from behind. For a long time there wasn't any answer and I thought of leaving, of going downstairs to see Carl's mother or father in the restaurant. Then I heard footsteps come to the door and the porch light went on and the door opened.

I remembered her face though I could no longer remember her name. Her dark eyes were like Carl's. She was a young woman now and she held a baby asleep on her shoulder, a white cloth spread over her shoulder and underneath the baby's face.

"Yes?" she said, the sound barely leaving her lips.

I wasn't sure what to say. I had thought Carl would come to the door. As though nothing had changed. He would laugh as he saw me. We would both then laugh to see each other again. It wasn't important what I said. But then it wasn't Carl and I had to say something.

"Is Carl here?"

She looked at me as though she hadn't heard what I said.

"Carl?" she said, the word softly spoken.

"I used to live not far from here. It was years ago," I said. "I just came back."

She didn't say anything but stood looking at me as though not knowing how to answer, and then she said simply and quietly, "Carl's dead."

I didn't hear her at first. I was going to say that I was sorry I couldn't remember her name, when her words opened like a wound in my mind.

60

"Carl's been dead for two years," she said.

"I'm sorry. I didn't know."

"Didn't anyone tell you?"

"No, no one told me. I'm sorry."

She waited again before she spoke, the light overhead casting her eyes in shadow.

"He drowned. Near Malibu."

She stood in the open doorway, the baby asleep on her shoulder. I could hear the noise from the restaurant below. I wanted to sit down. I held on to the wooden railing behind me.

"You want me to call Mama? She and Papa are downstairs," she said.

"No," I said. "It's all right."

"Is there something you want?"

"No, I don't want anything."

I started to turn away. Then I looked back at her and said, as though I was telling her I knew what had happened, "He's dead."

"Yes," she said.

We stood in silence for a moment and then she smiled an embarrassed smile and said good night and stepped back through the doorway but did not close the door. I said good night, too, and then I remembered her name.

"Good night, Rose," I said.

She stepped back out onto the porch. But I had turned away and had started down the stairs, counting the steps as I went. I felt her watching me as I turned back on the path between the restaurant and the garage that I remembered led out to the beach. The light from the back dining room flooded a little square of sand and I walked through the light and then into the darkness, feeling the soft sand pull at my feet. Here the beach was wide and I was tired by the time I reached the water. It was chilly and I turned my collar up against the sea breeze and put my hands in my pockets. Two hundred and eighty-seven steps to the water's edge. Two hundred and eighty-seven steps from the top of Carl's porch to where you couldn't walk any farther. I felt the ham sandwich in my pocket and took it out, carefully tearing it in half. I wrapped one half back into the napkin and put it back into my pocket for the morning. Perhaps it was always this way, I thought. Perhaps this is the way it was meant to be.

I went down to where the water touched my feet and looked at the waves breaking far off shore. Then I walked back up a little ways out of the water's reach and sat down on the sand and ate the sandwich, looking at the quiet ocean rolling gently over and back across the smooth sand. I wondered if anyone had ever tried to count the waves, which one it was that had rolled over Carl in that last moment of his life.

## 12

MAYBE THIS WAS THE WAY IT WAS meant to be just as it was the way it had always been, like some cruel joke played over and over again until nothing at all made any sense. I didn't know anymore what it was I was doing—if I had ever known—why I had come to sit alone on a dark beach, why things happened the way they had. It was like a nightmare I couldn't wake from. I had wanted to be somewhere where it was warm because it had always been so cold in the trailer I had never been able to sleep very well but had always lain huddled under the blankets waiting for morning so I could get dressed and go some place where it would be warm. And I was too young to know what was happening except that I had to hold onto myself, that I had to hold tight to the few pieces that were left before they too were lost somewhere.

Carl was dead. She had said that. Carl's dead. And one more piece was gone that I would never find again. The gull we had hit with a stone, it had been right here, and here we had sat watching it, not knowing at first whether it would recover or not, and how happy we were when it did recover and then flew off over the incoming waves, gradually climbing higher and higher. And how without saying anything to each other we never threw stones at birds again but only at the waves, trying to catch the crest of the wave just as it broke, the stone bouncing off the top of it. We had walked all along the beach scaling the old piers and exploring the rotting shacks we sometimes found on them, discovering the places where tramps had stayed, finding the empty wine bottles we would then throw into the sea, the light catching them before they were caught by the waves. Carl had been a good swimmer, far better than I. How could he drown? How was it possible? And yet it was true. He's dead, she had said. Rose, who no longer remembered me. Maybe I had killed him. If I hadn't come back I would never have known and he would still be alive, alive in me. Now death had taken his place, death that came before me, that followed after me, each day taking more and more of my world until I didn't know anymore where I could go that it wouldn't be there, too.

Whatever I was doing it was wrong. I knew that now. I couldn't go back because there was nothing to go back to. Whatever had been lost of my own childhood could never be recovered by going back to all the places I had been through. There were too many places and I would spend my life just looking for the life I had lost, like following a circle endlessly around and around never finding the beginning without finding there too the end. I thought again of Emile and of the book he had kept and of the crazy Armenian from whom Emile had first gotten the idea of writing a book of the things that were to be kept. I wondered if I could find the place where Emile's body had rolled out of the boxcar and if I went there could I find the book he had so carefully maintained and in which my name too must have been written. But then he had never known my name and it would be impossible to find that spot again as I didn't even know what state we had been in when it happened, when he died trying to catch a train that wouldn't have taken him anywhere and from where he would have to leave again. And even if I could have found the place deep in the weeds where his body had fallen what good would it do? So things would be remembered a little while longer is what he had said. But would they, would it have made any difference if everything was put down in a book, would they live any longer before death came and scattered the pages? Everything dies and is reborn to die again and in between there is the pain of birth only erased by the pain of death. The light dimmed slowly from my father's eyes. I remembered. He had been dying for years. What was it then that would be important if this was the way it would always be?

## 13

A SMALL RAIN HAD STARTED TO FALL as I got up and began walking along the beach. It was cold now and there were no lights to be seen anywhere. The tide was out and the waves were breaking closer in to shore. Far ahead I saw a shadow, like a ship run aground on the beach, and I walked toward it and came to an old pier jutting out over the water. It was ten or twelve feet over the beach at the water's edge. There was a wooden ladder built over one of the pilings but too many rungs were missing to climb it. I turned away from the water and walked along the pier until it was low enough to climb and then walked back out toward the water. There was a shack at the far end of the pier. I stood and looked at it for a moment, the rain now heavier, and then walked to the shack and went in. It was a relief to be out of the rain though it was as cold inside the shack as it was outside. The windows had been broken out and several boards were missing from the walls. I lit matches to see where I was and found a corner that looked dry. Someone else had stayed there at one time for there were bottles and scraps of paper and an empty burlap bag in the corner. I sat down and drew up my knees to my chest and put my head down and closed my eyes. I could hear the rain now hitting the shack all around me and several times the wind brought a fine spray in through the windows and over the back of my neck and hands. The pier moved with the waves, back and forth an inch or two at a time, the old piles creaking between the breaking of the waves. Later that night I imagined the pier falling into the waves, and trying to swim in the dark water, not knowing which way was land, not caring after a while, feeling peace overtake the terror of drowning, the dark waves over-head as silent as clouds moving across a brilliant sky.

"We're moving again, Carl."

"No kidding?"

"That's what Mother said. We've got to move again."

"Where to?"

"I don't know."

"Boy, I wish you could stay."

"So do I."

"Your father having trouble again?"

"I guess so. He's been pretty sick."

"Maybe you could stay with us. I could ask."

"No. There's too much for me to do at home."

"What about school?"

"I don't know. I guess I'll go to another."

"You can come back again, can't you?"

"I don't know."

"I mean later on."

"Sure, I'll come back later on."

I stayed there until morning, the rain no longer falling but the sky gray and heavy with clouds. The wind was strong and the pier shook and swayed as though at any moment it would fall into the waves breaking beneath it. I took out the rest of the sandwich and ate it.

There was enough light now to dimly see the inside of the shack. It was about eight feet square and was built onto the piles that came up at the end of the pier. There was a door at the ocean end of the shack that was now boarded shut, boards that had come from one of the walls, but looking through the window next to the door I could see the remains of wooden steps going part of the way down to the water; the rest of the steps had been broken off, the last step hanging down by a single nail and nearly touching the water as the waves swelled swiftly and silently beneath it. I looked at the sky; it would rain again soon. The gulls had already gone in to shore. I counted the money I had left, going over it again and again, knowing it would not last long. Nothing seemed to have worked the way I thought it would, the way I thought it might have worked; and it was cold. I couldn't escape the cold.

Carl was dead. Who else would be dead if I came to

see them, asking if they remembered me? What would happen if I went to other places I had lived, looking for what had been lost? What if I found only death? What would I do then? I thought again of Mexico. Whitaker had said it wasn't good in Mexico. But maybe it would be for me. It would be warm there, and it would be going on again. There would be peace in that, going where I had not gone before. I could get a job. There were, I was sure, American companies and one of them would give me a job. I could work. I would know no one, no one would know me. I could work quietly and carefully and feel my way slowly until the day came when it would be better, when I could begin to understand some of the things which had happened. It would be good that way, it would be like being born again.

There was a sound behind me and I turned around in time to see a man holding a plank high above his head and then I saw the plank come down on me again and again, but I didn't see the man's face, only his arms, white bare arms, as the plank hit me over and over on my head until I couldn't remember anymore except hands going through my pockets and then being lifted and shoved through a window and falling for what seemed like forever through the darkness.

# 14

AWOKE IN DARKNESS AND LAY THERE
listening to the silence of the trucks speeding down the
highway and it was as though the trailer was parked in
the middle of a long dark tunnel and the trucks would
enter at one end and race past shaking the trailer each
time they came and then rush on to escape the tunnel
pulling in darkness and silence after them and I awoke in
darkness and listened to my sister's breathing in the bed
next to mine and listened too to my own breathing and
I could still smell the odor of kerosene in the air though
it was faint now as the stove always burned itself out
sometimes during the night and I lay cold and huddled
under the blanket my knees drawn up to my chest you
must keep trying I thought all the time listening to the

mystery of my being alive in the moving darkness that touched my open eyes and my body as I turned around and around in it and I could reach out and feel the darkness itself lying in bed my arms extended upwards as though I were holding up the night from pressing too tightly on me until my arms began to tingle and then grow tired until they were no longer extended up into the dark over me but rotated slowly around and around until they dropped like dead weights though I could still feel them tingle almost like little bells were being played under the skin of my arms until I couldn't move them anymore but lay listening to the music of my body and I could hear far away the rushing sound of something entering the tunnel and I listened to it come until it broke upon me and then swept past me down the dark tunnel going out from my eyes I could see the dark just as I could hear the silence and I thought again that I must keep trying and I tried to reach out for anything to keep myself from falling through the tunnel but I couldn't raise my arms anymore because they were too tired and the tingling like little bells under the skin was so strange I could never understand and once had asked Mother why that happened and she had smiled as though it were a secret only she understood she said it was because they were asleep and she would lower her voice when she said that and then whisper shhh we mustn't wake them and so I never knew why that was I must keep trying to understand the mystery of being alive in darkness as though I were a light shining out in all directions like the sun in space turning around and around and the dark pressing in upon me a great weight and I wanted to get away from it and I got up from the bed and carefully got dressed and went outside quietly closing the trailer door behind me and walked out into the field next to the trailer park and down to the pond at the bottom of the field and it was cold and I thought if I ran I would get warm but my legs were too heavy to run and when I got to the pond it was still and dark like a hole had opened in the earth and I was standing there at the side of it looking into the hole that went down through the earth like a tunnel and at the far end of it I could see faint little lights and if I let myself go and were to fall into the hole I would fall into the lights which were stars in space around me falling forever through the tunnel of darkness before me and I felt myself being carried by invisible forces into the night lifted up as though my body no longer belonged to me or to the earth and I was happy then for a moment because I was entering the darkness where everything was peaceful and quiet and I could no longer smell the kerosene of the trailer or hear the rushing of the trucks on the highway that would one night run us all down because nothing mattered anymore but being carried along in the cool night oh god I thought over and over again oh god oh god oh god

## 15

I WAS LIFTED UP AND THROWN AGAINST
the pier with a force that brought me back to consciousness. I could remember nothing but fighting for breath
and trying to hold on to the dark column which held
up the pier overhead. My arms were heavy and they
ached and it was hard to lift them but I managed to
bring them up and wrap them around the pile I had
been thrown against. I clung to it breathing in great
gulps of air and tasting the salt of the ocean water and
the blood which ran down my face and into my mouth,
my heart pounding in my throat with small explosions
of pain. I held onto the pile with my arms and legs and
between the sounds of the breaking waves I heard footsteps overhead walking away from the shack and I re-

membered then that I had been thrown out of the shack and into the ocean from the end of the pier. And I knew why. I let go of the pile with one arm and felt under the water the outside of my pocket where I had kept my money. It was gone. I worked my hand into the pocket but it was empty, even the change had been taken. I looked around me but could see little except the gray beach a long ways off. I had lost my glasses. For a moment I wanted to let go. I wanted to stop and not go on anymore. My body was numb with cold. But my head was clearing and when another wave came I let it carry me along and made for the next pile, and then hung on to it and rested, waiting for another wave to come to take me farther in.

It was a long time before I made the beach. I was shivering badly and my chest was tight so that it was hard to breathe. I felt the top of my head and at the back where I had been hit and could feel an open cut and several swellings and could feel too the blood that was still running down the side of my face. I knew I had been hurt and I was scared that if I didn't get out of the cold soon something worse would happen.

There were houses all along the beach. I had trouble focusing my eyes and couldn't see whether the windows of the houses were shuttered or not. They looked dark and closed, like driftwood piled high along the outermost reach of the water. I started to walk toward one of the houses. The sun had not yet cleared the horizon though it had been light for what seemed like a long time. I looked around the beach for the man who had hit me and taken my money but could see no one; even the gulls were gone. The tide was coming in now and the beach was smooth, long gray lines of softly curling waves spread out in either direction as far as I could see. My whole body was shaking and I felt as though if I fell I wouldn't be able to get up again.

The house in front of me was dark. There was a large No Trespassing sign on the stone wall next to the iron gate. The gate was locked but it was not high. I looked around me to the deserted beach and then climbed the gate and stood inside a quiet, sand-filled yard. A small swimming pool, empty of water with sand filling its corners and all along one side, was enclosed by the wall which ran to either side of the house. I went up to the door and knocked on it. There was no answer. I looked for a doorbell and found it and pushed it several times but heard no sound from beyond the door. I knocked again, louder this time, waiting several minutes for an answer, and when none came I took off one of my shoes and with the heel broke the glass panel next to the door and reached in and opened it.

It was dark inside the house as the door swung open. The curtains were drawn. I stepped inside and it smelled musty as though the windows hadn't been opened for a long time. I took my other shoe off and left them both by the door and then closed the door quietly behind me. Then I stood there and waited.

After a few minutes I could see the outline of furniture, of other doors, of a flight of stairs. My head no longer bled but the blood had dried on my face and neck and it pulled at my skin when I turned my head. I stood leaning against the closed door, listening to the quiet of the house, watching the shadows slowly retreat into the silent air around them. Then carefully I took a step forward, and then another, and listening all the time for other sounds I quietly explored the house I had entered, moving from one room to another until I had made certain I was alone.

There was a laundry room next to the kitchen and I took off my wet clothes and left them there and took a blanket from a linen closet next to the laundry room and wrapped it around me. I was no longer cold. I felt safe in the silent house. But my head hurt and I knew I had to lie down. In the bathroom next to a bedroom on the ground floor I looked at myself in the mirror and was puzzled by what I saw. Someone else looked at me, someone I no longer knew. He was tired and his face was drawn, his eyes bloodshot and the lids swollen. His face was dark with blood that had dried to a brown stain over the side of his face and over his right ear and down his neck and onto his shoulder. I looked at him and thought of Whitaker and of the birthmark Whitaker had across his face. I opened the glass cabinet so I could not see the face staring at me, and then carefully washed the blood away from my face with my fingers and felt the cut again on the back of my head. There were several cuts I found, though none of them seemed to be deep, but the whole top and back of my head was covered with swellings and my right ear had a cut on it that was deep and that began to bleed again as I tried to wash the blood from it. I didn't turn on the light, and I ran the water slowly in the sink and tried to make as little noise as I could.

There was a bottle of aspirins in the cabinet above the sink and I took three tablets and then went back to the kitchen. The laundry room was just off the kitchen. I saw my clothes lying like a dark stain on the floor in front of the washing machine. I would wait until the traffic on the highway became heavier before I washed them, although I was sure no one could have heard whatever sounds I made. But I didn't want to take any chances. I was very dizzy and it was hard to think.

The refrigerator was empty and so were most of the kitchen cabinets. It looked as though the house had not been used for some time. But I found a few cans of soup in one of the cabinets and I opened one of them and put the contents in a pan and put the pan on the stove and turned on the gas. But the gas didn't work and for a moment I thought it must have been turned off until I began to smell it. I turned the burner off and tried another. But it, too, didn't work. I looked in all of the drawers in the kitchen for matches but couldn't find any. Then I remembered my clothes by the washer and the matches I had in my coat pocket that I had taken from the gas station. I went and got them and looked for any that might be dry enough to light but they were wet, so I went back to the stove and ate the soup from the pan cold.

And standing in front of the stove, I thought of going back. It had been a mistake, a bad beginning just as it had always been a bad beginning. No matter what was started, tried, it had never worked. What made me think it would be any different now? But yet I knew I couldn't go back to something that never was, and I was frightened now by what I had seen in the mirror. Someone else had taken my place, and I could remember his name better than I could recall my own. "Jason Canen," I had said. But I had been wrong, sitting in Eckburton's car, thinking it would make a difference. The young face I remembered was still beneath the older face I had seen in the mirror; and I thought of death again, of Eckburton, of Emile running by the side of the train, of Carl.

It was still light when I awoke. My head hurt badly now and I had trouble focusing my eyes. I took three more aspirins from the bottle in the bathroom and then went into the laundry room and put all my clothes into the washer and turned it on. I couldn't find any soap. Then I went back to the door I had first entered and looked at my shoes. The toes had curled and one shoe had come apart at the sole.

I kept the blanket around me and walked about the house. There were three other bedrooms on the second floor, another bathroom, and a small room with a desk in it and several shelves of books and a large armchair. The room faced the highway, as did one of the other bedrooms, and I could see the highway from the two windows of the room. There were tan curtains drawn over the windows and I pushed them aside from one of the windows and looked down. Long shadows fell across the highway. It was heavy now with traffic. I thought it must be around six o'clock and the cars were full of people returning from work. I looked at the cars for a long time thinking that it would be good to be going some place. I couldn't remember what day it was.

In one of the desk drawers there was a large blue notebook with a stiff paper cover, the kind I had once used in school. I took it out of the desk and looked through it. The pages were blank except for the first three. These were filled with neat columns of figures in what appeared to be an account of household expenses. I took the three pages out of the book and left them on the desk. Then I sat down at the desk and wrote on the first new page how Emile had made the fire that night and how he had kept a book so that things would be remembered. Under that I wrote what the name Los Angeles meant.

It had begun to get dark as I went back through the bedrooms on the second floor. I wanted to see if I could find another pair of shoes and I had to look while there was still enough light outside. I didn't want to turn on the house lights. I found a pair of tennis shoes in the last bedroom I searched, in a box on a closet shelf. They were a little too large for me but I could walk in them. I took a page out of the notebook and wrote on it how my shoes had been ruined and that I needed a pair of shoes. I wrote that I was sorry I couldn't leave any money to pay for them, and that I was sorry I had to break a window to get into the house. I put the note on top of the box and left it on the desk in the small room and then went downstairs. I put my clothes in the dryer. I opened another can of soup and ate it directly from the can and listened to the soft rumble of the dryer as my clothes tumbled about inside it.

I had been gone for five or six days. I couldn't remember how many days it had been; and now I had no money. I thought of Emile again, of going from one place to another, of wandering all over the country. I wondered if this was the way it was going to be. It would be good to have some place to go, to belong somewhere. Like the cars on the highway. They were all going some place. And yet, would it make any difference?

The dryer turned softly in the quiet of the house, and listening to its hum it was some moments before I was conscious of the telephone ringing.

## 16

THE TELEPHONE RANG FOR A LONG time before it stopped, and when it did I could hear my heart beating over the quiet hum of the dryer. When my clothes were dry, I quickly dressed and left the house the way I had entered. I climbed the gate again and walked along the upper beach in the soft sand until I was far from the house and then went back to the highway. The traffic had thinned now and several cars had their lights on, though it was not quite dark. I raised my hand, standing on the side of the highway and where I could jump if I had to, and then waited for a car to stop to take me away from Los Angeles. I thought again of Mexico, like some promised land.

But the cars kept going by, one after another. I began

to walk south along the highway after a while. It was darker now. I kept well to the side of the road, remembering what had happened before. Every once in a while someone on the passenger side of a passing car would look at me as the car they were in sped by, but none of the cars slowed down. I kept thinking of Whitaker, of the blood I had seen on my face. Everything was beginning to fall apart, and I was scared of what would yet happen. I no longer looked at the cars but just continued to walk, singing to myself the old song I always sang when things were bad.

I had to get away, away from everything. I thought again of Mexico and wondered how I could get there without any money, without any money at all, and what would happen once I got there, if I could make it that far without any money. There was never enough money. Toothaches because there was no money for dentists, hunger because there was no money for food.

I turned around again and faced the traffic, moving closer to the edge of the highway, and raised my hand, my thumb extended behind me, and began counting the cars as they passed. It was too dark now to see into them, to see whether they saw me or not. I kept seeing my mother's face, her lips set firm because of her aching teeth.

It was an old prewar Plymouth sedan which finally pulled off the highway, and I was still conscious of the stiffness in my left ankle when I ran to where it had stopped. The man inside the car was alone and I got in next to him and closed the door behind me. The car smelled of beer and of cigarette smoke. I turned to the

82

man and thanked him for stopping but he had already put the car in gear and had pulled back onto the highway. He didn't speak until the car was going fast again. Then he said, "How far you going?"

I answered without a thought. "Mexico," I said.

He looked over to me and then back to the road, and then said, "Can you drive?"

"Yes," I said.

He looked back to me again and at the notebook I held on my lap.

"Is that all you've got?"

"Yes," I said.

I could feel the car slow down a little.

"What about your things? Mexico's a long ways away."

"I don't have any," I said.

"Are you in trouble?"

"No," I said, and then I told him a little of what had happened. I told him about catching the train that day in Minnesota, of meeting Emile and of how Emile had died with me watching him inside the freight car, of being robbed of my money and thrown off the pier, of how I wanted to go some place where it was warm because I didn't like the cold. I told him I didn't like Los Angeles and that I had made a mistake going there. I told him I had made a lot of mistakes so far.

He didn't answer me for a long time after that but I could feel the car increase its speed again. He lit a cigarette.

"I work in Mexico," he said. "It's where I'm going now."

For a moment I couldn't believe what I had heard.

The car was loud and the sound of the engine filled the inside of the car and I wasn't sure what the man had said. I didn't believe in luck or in coincidence or that things could sometimes be very easy if you happened to be in the right place at the right time. Nothing had ever happened that way before.

"Can I ride with you?" I asked.

He looked at me again. I couldn't see his face very well. The lights from the dashboard were out.

"That's where I'm going. If you can drive, you're welcome to come along."

I sat back in the seat. "Thanks," I said. "I'd like to."

He put out his hand. "What's your name? Mine's Neil McAllester." I could feel the calluses on the inside of his large hand.

"Jason Canen," I said. Then suddenly I remembered the face in the mirror and the blood I had washed off and Whitaker's birthmark. But McAllester spoke again, his voice quiet and relaxed.

"You can drive when we get to the border."

"How far is that?"

"About four hours, more or less."

He looked back over to me and said, "You can earn your way by doing half the driving. I work out of Mexico City and have a Mexican labor permit. We shouldn't have any trouble at the border. There are Mexican plates on the car. You pretend you're asleep in the back seat. I come back and forth often enough to know some of the immigration inspectors. I'll tell them you're my son. There shouldn't be any trouble. I have a son not much younger than you. We're separated, my wife and

84

me, but I come up often to see the kids. I've a girl, too, but younger. How old are you?"

"Seventeen," I said.

"The truth?" he said.

"Yes," I said.

"You look younger," he said.

We drove on for a while in silence. Then he asked, "You really lose everything back there?"

"Yes," I said.

"That's rough. You've got to watch out for tramps."

I thought of Emile again, and of my father, remembering now his face, and of the book I held on my lap. But I didn't want to say anything. I knew that as long as we were moving it would be all right.

## 17

LT WAS AFTER MIDNIGHT WHEN WE reached the border. We had stopped just before then for gas, and for coffee and sandwiches, and afterwards I got into the back seat and lay down with a blanket over me. At the border we had to wait for a bus to go through first and I was afraid something would happen, that they would find out I didn't have any papers or money, and I would be sent back. But I didn't say anything to McAllester. At the cafe where we had stopped earlier, I hadn't wanted to order anything because I didn't have any money and I wasn't sure what McAllester had meant when he said I could earn my way by doing half the driving. I was just going to wait for him to eat. But when I didn't say anything to the waitress, he told her to bring me the same thing he had ordered. His face was deeply lined and brown, as though he had spent all his time out of doors, and his hair was thick, like a wire brush, and had begun to turn gray. We sat at the counter of the cafe and McAllester leaned on the counter on his elbows, his hands folded in front of him. His hands were large and the backs were covered with black hair.

"You're taking quite a chance," he said.

He hadn't looked at me but sat with his head bent down, his eyes searching the backs of his hands. His fingers were short and thick and the knuckles were scarred. "You sure you want to go on?" he said. "The border's just ahead."

I didn't know what to say and so I said nothing. I wasn't hungry and I ate the sandwich slowly. McAllester looked at me after a moment when I hadn't answered him, his eyes gray and hard. "He gave you quite a beating, didn't he?" he said.

"Yes," I said. "But it's all right now."

"Good," he said. His eyes seem to soften as he looked back at his hands. Then he picked up his sandwich and began eating. "I guess you know what you're doing," he said.

We finished eating in silence. I kept thinking of the cafe where I had been sick and where afterwards I had met Whitaker. That seemed like a long time ago now. Then I turned to McAllester and spoke to him, the words spilling out quickly and quietly while a knot tightened in my stomach. I told him I didn't know where I was going or what I was doing but that things were bad where I had been and I was trying to get away from where things had always been bad and I just wanted to start all over again. Maybe it was wrong, maybe there wasn't ever any beginning but only a continuation of what had always been, but I didn't know enough to know that then. I had to do something. I didn't want to go where I had been before because I had tried that and it hadn't worked, and I had been to too many places already. I thought Mexico might be different for me. It would have to be. I didn't even know the language.

McAllester finished his coffee and stood up, a great hulk of a man standing over me. "Fair enough," was all he said. He paid for the meal and we went out.

I lay still in the back seat and I heard the guard come up to the car. McAllester spoke to him in Spanish and the guard seemed to know him. They talked for a few minutes. I couldn't understand what they said. Then the car moved ahead slowly and stopped again. Another guard came out and the two guards and McAllester talked again, their voices soft. I kept my eyes closed and didn't move. The knot in my stomach grew tighter. Then the two guards walked away and the car moved forward again, slowly at first and then faster, and I knew everything was all right. But I didn't get up from the back seat until McAllester leaned his head back and said that I could relax now, we were in Mexico and on our way to Mexico City. Then he laughed, a deep resonant laughter that drowned out the sound of the car, and held up a handful of letters. "The mail service between here and Mexico City is terrible. I'm to mail these when we get there."

I sat up and looked out the side window. McAllester drove slowly until the lights of the town were behind us. When we got on to the main highway again he pulled over to the side of the road and got out.

"Let's see you handle it from here," he said.

I got out and we switched places. I had trouble bringing the seat forward. McAllester put his feet against the back of the front seat and pushed and the seat slid forward an inch at a time. When it was adjusted so I could see and could reach the pedals, I started the engine.

"She's all yours," he said.

I put the car in gear and we jerked forward.

"You'll get used to it. Just take it easy. We've a long way to go." He was lying on the back seat, his knees up, the blanket folded for a cushion under his head.

The car was in third gear now and we were moving faster, the headlights pushing against the darkness.

"There's a bottle under your side of the seat. Hand it back if you can find it," he said.

I reached down and felt under the seat and my hand touched the bottle. I brought it up and passed it back to McAllester. By its weight, it felt as though it was full.

"You wake me when you get tired, all right?"

"All right," I said.

I heard him unscrew the cap of the bottle.

"We stay on this road all the way to Santa Ana," he said. "Then we head south on route 15 toward Hermosillo." He took a drink from the bottle and I could smell the sweet smell of the whiskey.

"It's a long trip," he said.

I settled back in the seat a little and brought the car up to just under sixty. The car kept wanting to go off to the right of the road and I held tightly to the wheel and could feel my hands beginning to perspire. We were alone on the highway. I could see no lights ahead of us.

And I remembered a long time ago. Sitting in the old Pontiac, I used to turn the steering wheel when the car sat out behind the restaurant, first one way then another, pretending I was driving. I couldn't see over the wheel then but I thought that if I brought a pillow out from the motel room I could put it under me and then I would be able to see. But I didn't know how to work the pedal then or the gearshift lever, except I knew from watching Father that the lever had to first go down and then go up and then go down again. And I did that, sitting in the old Pontiac, wondering how we would all get to where we were going if Father died and I would have to drive the car. I thought that if I sat there long enough and pushed the gearshift lever first up and then down I would be able to learn the mystery of how it worked and I would be able then to take care of everybody because I knew that if Father died it would be up to me to take care of everybody, just as Mother said.

McAllester spoke again.

"Do you know any Spanish?"

"No," I said. "I don't know any Spanish."

"I didn't either, when I first came down here."

He took another drink and then put the cap back on the bottle. "That was about five years ago. Just after the war. We had just split up, my wife and me, and I got a job with an American construction company. I've been here ever since."

I kept thinking of the Pontiac, of how the lever went up and then down, of the radio that had never worked, of the dent in the trunk lid that was there when we bought the car to begin the trip from one place to another.

"It's easy to learn."

"What?" I said.

"I said, 'It's easy to learn.' Spanish."

"*Adios*," I said. "I know *adios*."

McAllester laughed. "That's a hell of beginning," he said.

## 18

I DROVE ALL THAT NIGHT, NOT WANTING
to wake McAllester, and wanting to think; and yet it
was hard to think of the future, of what I was doing. I
was being swept along by the past, trying to outdistance
it, while it remained forever just behind me. I kept looking into the rearview mirror thinking I saw the old trailer
behind us. It was not there, and yet each time I looked
I thought I saw its dark shadow behind us, like a giant
hand ready to come down upon the car fleeing before
it. I wondered if I would ever escape.

The stars were hidden by the overcast sky. It was cold
in the car. I found the switch for the heater and turned
it on. Only a few cars came toward us out of the darkness; none was going into it as we were. Occasionally the

moon shone faintly through the clouds, or just behind them there was a pale yellow glow as though a dim lamp hung behind thick curtains. But it only served to accentuate the darkness into which we drove. Old memories troubled me.

"Where are we going?" I had asked.

"Hush now, and try to sleep."

"But where are we going?" I kept asking.

"Home," she had said.

"Where's that?" I asked.

"Hush," she said. "It's late."

"But there's our home, right behind us," I said.

And I would sit up on my knees in the back seat and stare out the back window and look at home shaking and bumping along behind us, swaying like the tail of an animal about to spring, the dim light of the moon reflected in its one small front window.


My hands were dry now and the knot in my stomach was gone. The sound of the engine was peaceful, promising that there would be something at the end of the road this time.

There was always the promise. It was, I knew, what made everything possible.

I had never seen it so dark, as though all the lights in the world were extinguished; and we were pushing against the darkness now, going further and further into it. The lights of the Plymouth hung before us like a canyon into which we plunged, the black road rushing under us like a swift river between the gravel banks. Now and again a stone marker came up to the right, its numbers slowly diminishing. I tried hard to think of what I was going to do, of how I would live. There had always been such a concern for money for food, money to pay for the expense of living, of keeping alive, and I couldn't think how it would be possible. I had taken quite a chance. McAllester was right. But I was too tired to care anymore. I thought again of the clearing where Emile and I had stayed, of the river in which I had washed my hands and sat next to while a fish fed in the pool behind a fallen tree, that this might be the way it would always be; and I felt sick again at the thought of trying to outdistance the hopelessness I carried in me.

The car swerved suddenly to the right and into the gravel of the shoulder. I brought it back again onto the road and tightened my hands on the wheel. I looked behind me but McAllester had not awakened. I turned off the heater and opened the side vent to let fresh air into the car. The blue notebook was next to me on the front seat. I reached over and picked it up and put it on my lap.

We were nearly out of gas when we came to a small town. It was beginning to get light, the sky in front of us gray. I pulled the car into a gas station and turned off the lights, and then the motor. I looked on the map McAllester had stuck up behind the visor and saw the town was Caborca. There was little of it to see at first—the station, a few old buildings coming together in the middle of the desert. The station hadn't opened yet. McAllester still slept, the bottle of whiskey on his chest and cradled under his arms. I stretched out my legs and closed my eyes.

94

We were both asleep when a man came over to the car and knocked on the window. He was small with straight black hair and a young face. I sat up and rolled the window down and the man spoke to me in Spanish. McAllester sat up then and asked me what was wrong.

"We're almost out of gas," I said.

McAllester rubbed his face and then got out of the car and spoke to the man. I started the engine and drove the car up to the single gas pump and the man began putting gas into the car. Then I got out and walked over to where McAllester stood.

"We're in Caborca," I said.

"Yes, I know," he said. "We've made good time."

"I thought I'd let you sleep," I said.

"Thanks. I needed it," he said. "I'll drive from here."

He went back to the car and opened the trunk and took out a five-gallon can and the man at the gas pump filled the can after he had filled the tank of the car. McAllester paid him for the gasoline and then stood talking to him for a few minutes, the man pointing to a dirty, shack-like house next to the station. The sun was just over the horizon, the sky still overcast. The land was flat and brown and quiet as though nothing were alive. A car passed the station coming from the direction we were going. It was the first car I had seen for several hours. The air was already warm.

McAllester called to me to come with him and we walked together to the old house and entered. There were three tables and a makeshift counter in the room and a woman who stood watching us as we entered. She was young and pregnant. McAllester spoke to her and I repeated the words he used and he laughed at the way I

95

pronounced them. We sat at one of the tables. The woman went into another room and came out again carrying two large cups of coffee which she put on the table. Then she left again without saying a word.

The stubble of beard on McAllester's face was gray and he looked older than last night. He drank his coffee holding the cup in both hands. The young woman came back with a plate of fresh rolls and butter. The butter had begun to turn rancid but the rolls were very good. She brought McAllester another cup of coffee. I didn't like black coffee and drank mine slowly.

"How often do you make the trip?" I asked.

"Once, twice a year. It depends. I go up to see the kids. They're big now. They don't remember me. I don't know why I do it. Love, I suppose. Maybe I won't much more."

"It's good for them," I said.

"I don't know. Maybe. Maybe not. I don't think it makes any difference. Not any more. It's hard to know."

He reached into his pocket and brought out a handful of Mexican paper money. The bills were dirty and looked old as though they had been in circulation for a long time. The young woman stood a little ways away watching as McAllester put several of the old bills on the table.

We went back to the car and McAllester got in behind the wheel and pushed the seat back. I got in next to him. The man who had given us gas still stood by the pump watching us. I waved at him as we left the station but he didn't wave back.

When we were on the road again McAllester said,

"Those were Indians, back there at the station, the man and his wife. They're good people, Indians, among the best I've ever known."

I was beginning to feel dizzy, a pain at the back of my head. The sun was still hidden by the clouds. We stopped again on the other side of the town. It was larger than first I thought. McAllester bought some fruit and a loaf of round bread and a bottle of spring water at an open market. I stayed in the car. My head hurt and I didn't want to move, though I didn't say anything to McAllester. There were a few women at the market and a small, naked boy who stood a little ways away from the car, staring at me.

It was warm now and we rolled the windows down as we started to drive again. The wind washed into the car through the open windows lifting the collar of McAllester's blue shirt and blowing my hair.

"How're you feeling?" he asked.

"Fine," I said. "I feel fine."

"Your head looks better," he said.

"I should have been more careful," I said.

"Things happen. As I said, sometimes it's hard to know."

"Yes, it is," I said.

I picked up the book and held it on my lap, fingering the edges.

"There are a lot of Indians in Mexico, pure Indians descended from the Aztecs; maybe twenty–thirty per cent of the country. They're good people. Poor as hell, most of them. A few work for me. They're quiet people, hard to know."

97

"What do you do?"

"Build roads, viaducts, bridges. Water's a problem here. You'll see. It's what I did in the army. Civil engineering. I've gotten to like the country. It would be easier to fly up to L.A. but I like the drive. And I like the earth. I don't like flying. I was in a plane crash once. In the service. We were being transported from North Africa to Sicily and the plane lost its landing gear just as it touched down. It was at night and most of us were asleep. Two men were killed, and a lot of us were hurt. I broke both collar bones and my jaw and several ribs. I've never wanted to fly after that, and was scared as hell each time I did. I haven't been in a plane for five years. Being that close to dying was enough for me."

"I've never been in a plane," I said.

## 19

WE HAD STOPPED FOR GAS AT
Santa Ana and were now headed due south through the
desert of Sonora. We had eaten the fruit along the way.
McAllester had brought out a canvas water bag from the
back of the car at Santa Ana and had filled it and hung
it on the front of the car.

"We may need that later," he said.

Then we drove on for a long time and I fell asleep in
the front seat. It was hot now and half asleep I felt my
shirt sticking to the back of the seat. The pain in my
head had gone but it was replaced by a numbness so
that I felt as though I were in two worlds. I tried to
watch the flat, barren landscape, to get a feeling of the
country I had entered and which was different from

anything I had ever known, but it was hard to focus my eyes and they kept closing and I saw the world as though in a dream; and then I slept.

I had been walking for a long time on a path that I had wanted to follow, though I didn't know why, through a field where plants and flowers were of shapes and colors new to me. Birds circled over my head, for it was a clear day and the sun shone brightly and I walked through a field of tall grass of an intense green wanting only to come to the end.

The path I followed was clearly marked, and where the grass was parted by clear-running brooks that crossed the path there were smooth and ample stones which the water gently ran around, and on which I easily stepped to the other side.

Butterflies danced before me on the path, delicate white and golden butterflies that knew no fear of me but danced in my face and rested on my shoulders. My heart was filled with a painful joy as I walked because I knew a beautiful world waited for me at the end of the path and I would have only to follow it through the green field and over and down the soft hills to come to what I knew was waiting for me at the end.

And I had never been as happy as I was then, a happiness like pain touched all of my body and I could think of nothing but of where the path would lead.

Dangerous cliffs fell to my left and to my right a range of mountains rose to the clouds. But the path lay between the cliffs and the mountains and the birds followed me still, dipping and circling over my head, their song filling my ears with music and laughter so that I cried with the unbearable happiness of what I felt would soon be mine and could express in no other way but through my tears.

Before me there lay a white boulder that as I approached closer I saw to be an old man dressed in white robes and sitting on the ground by the side of the path

and I stopped and said hello and asked if this was the path that led to the beautiful world

but he only looked at me and said nothing as though he were a statue carved from white stone

and I turned my back on him and went my way again along the path

for he was but one more strange and unknown thing I had seen that day and I thought no more of him

because I was anxious to come to the end of the path for I was beginning to tire and the sun was warm

but the path was long and turned this way and that through the tall grass

and I came at last to a place where the path separated into two paths and I stopped not knowing which one to take

I looked for the birds circling my head but they were now far above me and I could see no pattern in their flight which would tell me the way to go

I thought then that the heart is to the left and the heart could not be wrong and so I turned to the left and then once again I saw the old man sitting by the side of the path

and again I said hello to him and I asked him another time if this was the path to where all things lived

but again he only looked at me until I couldn't stand

the pain I saw in his eyes and I turned and stumbled along the path once more knowing it could not be wrong because my heart had told me to go the way I had gone

then once again I was alone and the path was no longer clear but full of brambles and rocks and deepening ravines

I found hard to cross but crossed each one though they cut my body and tore my clothes

the streams were broader now and more difficult to ford and often I sank deep into the chilling water before I was able to get to the other side

but the sun was still in the clear sky and it dried my body and the air was warm and I was filled with the thought that soon I would come to the end of the path

and I wanted to shout the joy I felt and to call the birds to follow me though I could no longer see the way they had gone

and the butterflies that had danced even before the old man were also gone and the path itself no longer clear

but only the matted grass and broken branches there to show where someone else had gone before

and all that day I walked feeling no other need but to come to the end of the path I had taken where there would be rest and food and where there would be shelter from the night now spreading silently over the empty sky

and the streams were now broad rivers along whose banks I walked to find a shallow place to cross and crossing them I came to others where torrents of water poured angrily down the mountainsides and which I crossed with fear now felt for the first time that I would not reach the end of the path

and I pulled myself out of the ice-cold waters of the rivers I crossed unable to breathe for the water I had swallowed and damp for the sun was now fallen behind the mountains

but the air was dry and a warm wind blew the chill from my body and it filled my lungs with sweet air and after each river I crossed I was able to still go on

along the path though it was dimly seen in front of me

but my clothing was torn even further by the branches before me which I could not see because of the fading light

and I was tired from walking and having to cross the many rivers I crossed

which I knew was only one river forever bending before me

and I felt my happiness begin to leave me and as I walked I heard him drop by the side of the path and I called back to him to follow me

to follow me because we had not far to go

while I knew he remained by the side of the path until I saw him no more

then once again I saw the old man sitting by the path as he had sat before and I stopped again and looked at him and spoke my heart to him asking why he had not answered me before and asking him now if this was the way to go

if the path I traveled would lead to where I wanted to go

and telling him then that happiness was no longer with me

but the old man did not answer me and I became
angry because I had gone so far and was tired now to
where my legs were heavy beneath me
and I reached down to where he sat and shook him
hard by the shoulders
crying out to him again and again for him to give me
an answer
and the old man's head fell from his shoulders and
rolled like a pebble between my feet
his eyes staring up from the ground at me
and blood spilled silently from out his mouth like a
fountain from the heart of the earth

## 20

I WOKE UP SCREAMING BECAUSE OF THE pain in my head and saw McAllester bending over me. I was lying alongside the road in the shade of the car. The blanket was under me and I could feel the pebbles of gravel under the blanket. McAllester had the canvas water bag next to him and he wet a handkerchief which he then placed on my head. He looked down at me and smiled, his face worried, and I was sorry for that.

"You all right now?" he said.

I tried to speak but the pain in my head was too great and all I could do was to open and close my mouth.

"Don't worry, we're not far from Hermosillo. There's a hospital there. We'll make it soon. Just hang on."

I tried to say I was all right but the words wouldn't come to my mouth and so I raised my hand and waved it once or twice to show him I was all right.

The rear door of the car was open and McAllester lifted me up and put me on the back seat and then put the blanket over me. He rinsed out the handkerchief again and replaced it on my forehead. Then he got into the car and we started off again, my head throbbing to the sound of the engine.

Several times after that McAllester would lean back and ask if I was all right and each time he did his voice sounded farther and farther away. It was too far away I knew for me to answer. He could never hear me from the distance where I lay.


The sun shone through the window of the car and I closed my eyes but felt the sun burning into my face and I tried to move to keep the sun from my face and then I remember McAllester stopping again and picking me up from the floor of the car and putting me back onto the seat. And then driving again and all the time thinking of the old Pontiac and that we were all going on again with me sleeping on the floor of the car. Where are we going I kept wanting to ask, the words turning over and over in my mind, where are we going, where are we going, the words drowned out by the sound of the engine, leaving a trail of questions behind us on the road.

I was tired and wanted to sleep and I was being carried from the car, and people's voices were speaking a language I couldn't understand. There was a blur of lights and someone was looking into my eyes and I could smell the odor of tobacco on his breath, and then the odor and the lights went away.

Then it was quiet and for a long time there was no other sound but the sound of my breathing and the hum of a machine somewhere far away, and I tried to move but was too tired to move though I felt my body push against the sheet of a bed and I tried to remember what had happened and where I was. A soft light came into the room through thin white curtains by the side of the bed, and turning my head a little I saw the light golden and warm and filled with millions of tiny floating particles that floated in the silent air.

I awoke again and a man in a white shirt was standing next to the bed. I looked at him and could see the light behind him and I could feel myself move on the bed. The sickness had gone and I wanted to sit up but the man gently put his hand on my shoulder and held me back. He spoke to me in English, his voice low and kind, a small smile at the corners of his mouth.

"How are you feeling, *Señor* Canen?"

I lay back again, his hand on my shoulder.

"You have had a concussion. Those wounds on your head, how did you get them?"

"Someone hit me."

"Who?"

"I don't know."

"When did it happen?"

"Yesterday morning, I think. I'm not sure."

"How did it happen?"

"I don't know."

"You don't know?"

"Someone came up from behind me and hit me with a board."

"I see."

"He took my money."

"Was it here in Mexico?"

"No."

"What happened after that?"

"It's hard to remember."

"Were you sick? Did you vomit? Did you lose consciousness?"

"Yes, for a while. I lost my glasses."

"Then what?"

"I don't remember. I slept."

"You are lucky."

"Yes."

"You will be all right. I will see you again in the morning."

"What day is it?"

"Tuesday."

"How long have I been here?"

"Since yesterday."

"Then it must have been the day before."

"When you were hit?"

"Yes."

"Then you are very lucky."

"Yes; I know."

"I will see you in the morning."

"Doctor?"

"Yes?"

"The man who was with me, is he here?"
"No. He left. He is your friend?"
"Yes."
"He left money for you, and a notebook."
"What day is it?"
"Tuesday. You must rest now."
"Thank you. *Adios.*"
"*Sí; adios.*"

## 21

I SLEPT ALL THAT DAY AND THE NEXT, waking during the day only to see the soft light come in through the curtains and move slowly across the room, and in the night, when someone would be standing at the foot of the bed, looking at me, and then leave without a word. But there was no other memory. My head was wrapped in bandages and my left arm was taped to a narrow tray with a needle stuck into my arm and from it a clear plastic tube ran up to a bottle of colorless liquid suspended from a metal post by the side of the bed.

Two, perhaps three, days passed in this way, and then they took the needle out, and I was able to eat, and afterwards to sit in the sun on a small balcony next to the room. The hospital was new and had two floors and there was grass planted in front of the hospital and beneath the balcony where I sat and the grass was brown as though it had never been watered. I could see very little of the town but what I could see was old and silent as though nothing were alive but the cars which occasionally drove down the dusty street. The buildings were low and looked as if they had been carved from soft stone that was now beginning to crumble, and everything was a shade of brown or gray.

The doctor came to see me frequently, never staying long. I felt better now and after the second day in the sun I was able to walk back to the room without the nurse having to take my arm. Only the doctor spoke English. There was a constant odor of cigarette smoke about him, though I never saw him smoke.

On the following morning the doctor came with a man he said was from the police. The man wore a suit but without a tie and he did not speak English and the doctor quietly asked questions for him. The man from the police made notes of what I said on the back of an envelope he had taken from his coat, and when he was finished he put the envelope back into his coat and talked to the doctor. The doctor looked at me several times and shook his head when he looked back to the man from the police.

"What is wrong?" I asked.

"He wants to make sure that it did not happen here in Mexico," the doctor said.

"What did you tell him?"

"What you told me."

"And what does he say?"

"He wants to know how much money you have."

I started to say something but the doctor frowned and raised his hand and then walked around the side of the bed and opened a door in the metal cabinet that stood next to the bed. He took out the book I had taken from the house on the beach. I did not know it had been there all this time. I lay back on the bed and felt my heart beat faster.

"There is five hundred pesos here that your friend left for you," he said, and he gave me the book. I didn't know what to say. I opened the book and there was a note from McAllester written underneath what I had written about Emile.

You had better go back. I hope this helps. Sorry it can't be more. Good luck. Neil McAllester.

I read the note a second time and then looked at the doctor. The man from the police walked away from the bed and stood by the window, the light falling between him and the bed as though he had stepped into another room.

"He says it is all right," the doctor said. "But you cannot stay in Mexico. He will give you an exit visa. He says you are to go back."

I closed the book and looked at the doctor and then at the man from the police.

"When can I leave here?"

"Tomorrow."

"I feel all right now."

"Good."

The doctor stepped through the light and talked with the man from the police for a moment, and then they both left the room.

After they were gone I got up from the bed slowly and went out to the balcony, holding my hand to the wall, and sat in the sun. It was quiet on the street below. I opened the book and saw the money McAllester had left and read the note again. I wanted to write something down in the book but I didn't have a pencil and so I closed the book and leaned back in the chair and felt the hot sun on my face. It felt very good to be warm and to sit there feeling the sun on my face, and for a long time I didn't think about what the doctor had said or about anything but how good it was to sit in the sun. They had taken the bandages off my head except for two small bandages that were taped to the back of my head and from which the hair had been shaved.

The doctor came out to the balcony and leaned against the rail with his back to the light. I couldn't see his face because of the light though I could still smell the strong odor of tobacco about him.

"I was going to go to Mexico City," I said.

The doctor took a small piece of paper from his breast pocket. "Perhaps another time," he said. He handed me the paper. "That is your exit visa."

I looked at the paper and then put it in the book on top of McAllester's money.

"You must understand that Mexico cannot be responsible should something happen to you in our country. Five hundred pesos is less than fifty American dollars. It will not go far."

"I thought I could work."

He shrugged his shoulders. "It is possible, but it is not very likely that you would find work. You are young, you speak only English."

"What does the visa say?"

"That you have permission to cross our border. It was very careless of them to have let you in. But these things happen. We all know this. But it is best you go back. Does your head hurt?"

"No."

"That is good."

"Thank you for what you have done."

"I would do the same for anyone."

"Thank you anyway."

"I will see you tomorrow before you leave."

He left the balcony. The sun was very hot. An airplane, its wheels down, circled over the town like a black insect against the bright sky, and then quietly drifted down into the distance beyond the edge of the town. Then nothing moved. I opened the book and picked up the money McAllester had left for me. I wondered why he did it. I had never held as much money at one time before, and I counted it again and again trying to think of what I would do.

## 22

I DECIDED TO GET MY CLOTHES AND
leave that afternoon. I didn't want to wait for the next
morning when the man from the police might come
again and when I might then not have any choice. I sat
in the sun and waited, going over in my mind that I
would find the airport and that I would take a plane
for Mexico City. There would be enough money for
that, and enough would be left over so that I could live
for a while. And I would find McAllester. I would find
McAllester and I would somehow pay him back.

I waited until midafternoon and then took my clothes
from the closet next to the door of the room and put
them on. It felt good to be dressed again. There was no
one in the corridor outside the room. I walked down the

corridor to the stairs at the end and then down the one flight to the main corridor. A nurse sat at a desk just inside the front door. I would have to go past her to get out, or go back up the stairs and then find another way out of the building. I stood at the bottom of the stairs and looked at the nurse. She sat bent over a magazine, her black hair shining in the light coming in from the door behind her. A telephone rang softly across the hall and I stepped back up the stairs. The telephone continued to ring and the nurse called out a name as though expecting someone to answer the telephone. When there was no answer she got up and walked down the hall and went into an office. I stepped out into the corridor when I heard the door close behind her and went out the front door and down the stone steps to the street. The other side of the street was in shadow and I crossed the street and walked into the cool shadow and away from the hospital. At the first corner I turned and then stopped and looked back. There was no one on the street. I waited for a moment, watching the entrance to the small hospital, and then turned and walked away.

I walked for a long time toward where I thought I had seen the plane. The sun was low in the sky and long shadows fell over the dusty street until the gray buildings were no more than the sand hills around them. I was out on the edge of the desert again, my coat draped over my head to keep the sun off the back of my head. I kept looking behind me as though I were being followed, but no one came after me.

I came to a crossroads and stopped, trying to remember from which direction I had seen the plane. The sun was now just over the horizon and there seemed to be nothing but empty desert in front of me. An old gravel truck approached from the right and I waved at the truck to stop. There were two young men in the truck and when the truck stopped I shouted up to them over the noise of the engine asking which was the way to the airport. They looked at one another and then at me and so I said "aeroplane" and held my hands together as though my hands were a plane. The driver of the truck said something I couldn't understand but pointed behind him with his thumb, and the other man grinned and leaned out of the window as the truck started to move again and pointed back toward the way they had come. I watched as the truck drove away and then began walking again, and far off in the distance I saw another plane rise slowly into the setting sun.

It was dark when I came to the small airfield. A two-engine plane was parked in front of the terminal building and men were working on one of the engines. There were ten or twelve people waiting in the terminal, sitting on benches along the walls. The building was old and two large black fans hung from the ceiling between the lights, their blades turning soundlessly. Behind the ticket counter a young woman in a light green jacket was writing on a blackboard, her chalk sometimes squeaking across the board. The people along the walls watched her as she wrote.

I went up to the counter and waited for the woman to finish. She turned around, wiping the chalk dust from her fingers. I asked her for a ticket to Mexico City.

She spoke English, though not well enough for me to

understand everything she said. But I could not go to Mexico City that night. The plane only went as far as Tepic, stopping first at Culiacán. From Tepic I would have to take another plane to Mexico City. She pointed to the numbers on the blackboard behind her. In the morning, she said, because of the mountains. Then she wrote out a ticket for me and told me to wait, pointing to the benches along the wall. They were having trouble with the plane and it would be a while yet before it could leave. The plane was to have left at five o'clock. It was seven-thirty now and the plane was not yet ready.

I went over to a bench and sat down. I was tired and wanted to sleep. I looked out the open door and could see several men working on one of the engines of the plane, and the dark night beyond the field, and far away, a soft glow on the horizon that was the town I had left.

A little boy, leaning against the legs of an old woman who sat on the next bench, looked at me and smiled, then hid his face in the old woman's skirts. Her face was a dark reddish-brown and cracked like a dry lake bed. She looked at me too and then patted the boy's head as he peeked at me with one eye just above the old woman's leg.

The fans turned slowly, not moving the air but only throwing faint shadows that swept swiftly about the room. The little boy had lain down with his head on the old woman's lap while she sat, her eyes closed, her hands resting on the boy's head, her brown fingers gently stroking his black hair.

I counted the money I had left and put it in my pocket, and then read McAllester's note again, his handwriting large and filling the rest of the page on which I had written the few words about Emile and of what he had said the words Los Angeles meant.

How could I go back to something that never was? Where was there to go?

It was nine o'clock when the plane was ready, and the old woman woke the child asleep on her lap. But the boy was too tired to walk and he held onto her legs as the old woman stood, picking up a battered suitcase that had been tied around with rope. The boy then let go of the woman's legs and lay down on the bench again, and the old woman pulled at his arm telling him to get up. I walked over to where she stood. The other passengers in the room were going through the door to the plane parked in front of the terminal. I gestured to the old woman that I would carry the boy out for her and she smiled and said something and I saw that she had no teeth. I reached down and picked up the boy and together we went out to the plane.

The plane still hadn't started its engines. It was hot in the cabin, though it was only about half full, and the men took their jackets off and the women fanned themselves. The boy slept on a seat. The old woman sat next to him, her eyes closed again, her hands holding a string of black beads.

The engines started and for a long time we sat there without moving. Then the engines became louder and we moved forward in a wide circle and out to the runway. The plane came to a stop again, and the roar of the engines shook the plane and the plane seemed to be held back by some invisible barrier. Then the barrier

119

broke and the runway raced beneath us, black streaks streaming under the lights of the wings, the plane shaking violently as though being torn apart by the effort to get into the air. Then a small, almost imperceptible bump came and suddenly the shaking stopped, and the ground sank beneath us, the lights from the field like small faint fires soon to be out.

The boy slept still, and the old woman looked over to me and smiled and nodded her head. I breathed deeply, suddenly aware that I had been holding my breath.

## 23

THE SMALL PLANE ROSE HIGHER through the clear night until the bright stars were nearly within reach. I felt a dull throbbing in my head and leaned back against the seat, closing my eyes.

I had entered the darkness willingly. But I was tired of running away, and afraid of the darker world before me. Events had taken their own turn and I had followed them, leaving one world behind me and entering another.

I held tightly to the book on my lap, fingering the edges, putting my hand between the cool blank pages. Words tumbled like a waterway through my mind, spilling over the edges of the real world, washing it away.

So things would be remembered a little while longer.

He had said that, sitting in the clearing before the fire. So things would not be forgotten.

But nothing was ever forgotten. For a time perhaps, but not for ever. We carried with us all those things that had ever happened. They were not forgotten, only pushed beyond memory for a time. Like the scars we bore on our bodies, they would always be there.

"After the first death, there is no other," someone had said. But death did not come all at once. It came little by little. Each day taking more and more. A whole lifetime spent in giving to death, a little each day until everything was gone.

If nothing remained then nothing continued, nothing coming out of nothing to go back into nothing, and all the time where was the question why? What difference did it all make if it made no difference at all? It would be better to sleep, to lie down in the dark and sleep.

Others had found the answer in the stars, and placed heaven beyond them for the stars were always there, slender columns of light holding the peace of distant dreams. The promise never fulfilled was never broken. The truth being of nothing would always be true.

The plane banked gently, and looking down I could see the long coast line, the silent white waves breaking against the dark shore.

## 24

WE FOLLOWED THE COAST LINE
for a long time and I slept on and off, never knowing
how long I slept as I could see no change in what I saw.
It was late at night when we landed at Culiacán, but
how late I did not know. Most of the passengers got off,
including the old woman and the boy who was now
awake and who held on to the back of the old woman's
dark skirt as they walked down the narrow aisle to the
door at the back of the plane. I stayed in my seat,
watching a fuel truck drive up to the plane and then a
man climb onto the wing hauling the fuel line up to the
wing with a rope.

The field was dark and the terminal building was only
half lit. I could see a small group of people waiting in

front of the terminal, and then the little boy run away from the old woman and toward a man who bent down, his arms outspread to receive him.

Then they were gone and the field was empty except for the fuel truck and the man kneeling on the wing. The pilot had gotten off with the passengers. I could see him now walking around the plane with a flashlight. He talked for a while with the man on the wing, though I could not hear their voices, and then walked over to the terminal building and went inside.

I closed my eyes and tried to sleep. The plane for Mexico City was to leave at eight o'clock in the morning and we still had to fly to Tepic. There were three other people in the plane and they seemed asleep. It was colder now that the engines had stopped, with the door at the back of the plane open. I reached up to the overhead rack and felt for a blanket and found one and brought it down and wrapped it around me.

I used to lie awake at night in the trailer, the blanket pulled up over my head, waiting for morning to come. Sometimes I would get dressed early and go to the building in which the washing machines were kept because it was warm there and I would wait until it was time to go back to the trailer for breakfast and then get ready to go to school. I would stand with my arms wrapped around one of the water heaters, or sit with my back against one of them and read comic books which I had taken from the trailer and which other children in the park and I would trade back and forth until their covers were gone and some of the pages missing so that many of the stories had no beginning or end. There were always laundry rooms, sometimes with showers in them, and they were always the first place I looked for when we moved from one park to another. In one of them once there was a candy machine and if a wire was inserted up through the slot where the candy came down, and if the wire was carefully worked back and forth, it would sometimes release a bar of candy. For a while I was the only one who knew about it and who knew how to bend the wire so that it would work. Then later I had told other children about it and often the machine would be empty in the morning when I would come and I was sorry I had told others the secret I had learned.

Like the hole in the wall that didn't lead anywhere but which was deep enough to crawl into so that no one could see you. The hole was hidden behind some boxes next to an old building that was, I think, a warehouse. I was six or seven years old then and I found the hole one afternoon and crawled into it but was afraid to go too far and came out again and told other children what I had found. And then one day I came back to it wanting to go in again and to see how far back it went and when I came to it I saw that some one had boarded it over with strong boards I couldn't pull loose. For years after that I thought the hole was how you got out of the trailer park and that it was boarded over so that you couldn't get out.

The door of the plane closed behind me and I turned my head and saw the pilot come up the aisle, the flashlight stuck into his back pocket and still turned on so that the light bounced along the ceiling of the cabin as he walked past me and up to the front of the cabin.

In a little while the engines started again and we taxied out to the runway, the plane vibrating as it had before, and then shaking and bumping down the runway until it was airborne. Only this time I did not hold my breath.

I watched the field disappear, the lights of Culiacán going out after it, and then the bright darkness of the night with the stars seeming to touch the tips of the wings.

I remembered Joseph. We had played together as children, Joseph and I. I couldn't remember where it was because there were too many places, and after a while they all looked alike, but I remembered Joseph because, for some reason I never knew, he didn't go to school, though he was my age, or perhaps even older. He would often wait for me, just a little ways from school, and in the late afternoons we would walk home together. He wore a brace on one leg so that we would have to walk slowly coming home from school, other children often running past us, shouting at us as they ran.

Joseph collected things. Anything that appealed to him he picked up and saved to add to his collection. His pockets bulged with bottle caps, the foil from cigarette packages, pieces of colored glass. They would all go into his collection which he kept hidden from everyone else in a cardboard box under the trailer where he and his mother lived. But he never talked about it, the box he kept hidden from everyone, and it was a long time before I knew it was there. He showed it to me one day, the first of two times I ever saw it, an old egg carton nearly filled with the bits and pieces he had picked up.

A few things I recognized—a wire brush he had found on our way home from school one day, and a broken red top with string wrapped neatly around it. Joseph emptied his pockets into the egg box, dumping what he had found into it and then, kneeling down on one knee with his other leg stuck out oddly behind him, he would spread the contents around with his hands, so there would be room for more or perhaps to make sure that all his things were still there. Then getting up and turning his back on it he looked at me, full of pride for what he had found but not wanting to give it any importance by staying too long or even by talking about it, and limped off, away from the back of the trailer, but not going anywhere at all.

On Saturdays and Sundays, when there was nothing to do, I could always find Joseph by the dump in the field behind the trailer park. It was where all who lived in the park brought their garbage to leave for the crows and the rats to pick over, and Joseph watched it for hours at a time. He never talked about the dump, as though it was somehow an extension of his own box; but it was his, and I knew, when I came looking for him and found him there, that I came into his world, and that, as a guest, I did only what he did. Sometimes he would limp around the dump, often stumbling down the hill over which the garbage was thrown, to see how the dump might have changed since last he saw it. But he never took anything from it, and once when I had picked up the cover to a comic book, meaning only to look at it, he stared at me until I put the cover back where I had found it.

One day I came home from school and Joseph was

not where he usually waited for me. I didn't think anything of it because he did not wait for me every day,
though I always expected him and was happy when I did
see him there. But walking into the trailer park I saw
that his trailer was gone, and I ran all around the park
trying to find where he had gone or what had happened.
But no one knew. After supper that night I went out
to the dump, and there on top of all the garbage was
Joseph's egg carton sitting like a prize on top of a mound
of trash. I climbed up to it and looked inside and everything was there as I had seen it that once before, but
there too was the comic book cover I had picked up,
though it was torn now into several pieces.

# 25

THE SKY TO THE EAST HAD SOFTENED and the earth's dark shape formed dimly beneath it, like some huge animal slowly awakening. I needed to sleep and wished I could go somewhere where I could lie down and where there was no motion, no sound but just stillness. Names and faces, words from another time filled my mind. I held tightly to the book in my hands, its blank pages suddenly filled with words.

And Emile was speaking, the fire burning between us.

"He once told me he could tell when a man was going to die."

"How did he know that?"

"The eyes. You can always tell when a man's going to die by looking at his eyes. They don't really see what they're looking at. . . . He used to keep a book, too. The Armenian. That's where I picked it up. It was full of all sorts of things. . . . That's why he used to keep a book, so they'd be remembered, so they'd live a little while longer."

But all I could remember was the smell of Father's body as he lay dying in the back of the trailer. I couldn't remember his eyes then, what they were like, what it was he had sought those last three days as he lay there, his eyes fixed on the low plywood ceiling. What could they see when there was nothing to see? It didn't mean anything, all that he did, all that he tried to do. His leaving, his coming back, the post cards he sent from faraway places. It meant nothing at all.

The plane bounced in the air like a flat stone thrown upon water. "Goddamnit, goddamnit to hell!" I said loudly, suddenly aware of the sound of my own voice in the dark silence of the plane. The pages of the empty book rippled under my fingers.

And Carl was speaking, his voice full of excitement as we walked along the beach.

"Imagine taking a ship and sailing all the way to China, all the way across the Pacific. Boy, that's for me. And you can be first mate. We'll go all over. All the islands. I've heard there are thousands of islands they haven't even mapped yet. They found them during the war. Some of them are big, too, with people on them who don't wear anything because it's always too hot. All they do is fish and fool around, all day long. Boy, that's the life. I've got eight hundred dollars in war bonds. When I'm out of school, I think that's what I'm going to do. I'm going to sail around the world and find all those islands they haven't found yet. And if we run out of money, we can always haul copra."

"What's copra?"

"I don't know. Something you haul from one island to another. I read about it once. But there's lots of other things, too. We could take pictures and sell them to magazines, pictures of all the places nobody has ever seen. Magazines are always crazy for pictures."

And all that afternoon we threw stones at the waves, the red sun going down beyond the blue water, the light shining in Carl's eyes as we walked along the beach.

And Eckburton said:

"I get to thinking that maybe there isn't anything anyone can do about it, I mean about drinking and what kids have to go through to grow up, that maybe it's just something we'll have to go through like in the last decade we had to go through the Second World War. This decade has its own problems, too, and we're just going to have to live with them until everything's been worked out. . . . All the things that have changed in my life-time: the car, the airplane, the atomic bomb, practically everything we know. I tried to explain some of this to the kids and the girls understood right away but all Jimmy could do was shrug his shoulders as though the automobile and the airplane and the atomic bomb weren't important to our lives. . . ."

I put my head to the cool glass of the window and looked at the skeleton of hills faintly outlined on the horizon. I could see the shadow of my own face against the glass.

And Uncle Ben, showing me the hoofprints of deer by the side of the pool in the woods, one set larger and deeper than the other, and Ben saying that one set was made by a buck and the other by a doe, and putting my fingers in the prints and into the soft damp ground I could almost see the deer standing there. And later when I had come back by myself I found the prints still there by the side of the pool, and there were others then, too, prints of animals all around the edge of the pool. I had stayed there for a long time thinking about the deer, of living alone in the woods where it was quiet. The moon had come up over the trees, and like a face it reflected on the still water as though it were watching me, and I could not move because of it.

"Why have you come here?" it said.

"I wanted to get away," I answered.

"Away from your family?"

"More than that. No one is happy. I wanted to get away from where no one is happy."

"You can't do that here. Not now."

"But it is quiet here, and no one yells at me. I can be by myself."

"That is only because you do not understand."

"What is there to understand?"

"It is like that everywhere."

"Unhappiness?"

"No, it is not as simple as that. Life is the same for everyone."

"It is not true."

"It is true, only you do not understand."

"I don't want to believe that."

"You are too young to know."

"I don't want to know."

"Then come. Here is the pool. There is peace here."

"I don't want to die."

"Everything dies. Today, tomorrow. It is all the same."

"I don't want to die."

"Part of you now, part of you later. Today, tomorrow. It is all the same."

"No," I said, and I stood up by the side of the pool and threw a stone at the face in the water and it was gone.

At the end of that summer Uncle Ben killed a deer in the woods and hung its carcass to a branch of a tree by the cold cellar where it hung for two days before he skinned it.


The plane began a slow turn and I saw the airfield below us, a single landing strip running at an angle to a narrow blacktopped road, and farther away I saw a cluster of low buildings that I thought was Tepic. I saw no lights in the town, and only a few lights marking the landing strip. The sun was nearly up now so that lights were not needed. Then the plane banked again and went down, and telegraph poles, dark and slender in the distance, came up from the ground and rushed past us, and then the wheels touched down. I wondered if the same plane would go on in the morning or if there would be another. I saw two small private planes parked on the dirt next to the runway, though I could only see part of the field from where I sat.

The other passengers were awake and were talking to one another and taking things down from the racks overhead. I folded the blanket and put it back and then waited for the plane to come to a stop.

That was as far as we were to go. The three other passengers in the plane, the pilot and another man whom I had not noticed before but who came out of the forward cabin with the pilot, left the plane after we had all climbed down the short ladder. We went into the terminal building. I sat down on one of the wooden benches in the center of the empty room while the others continued through a door next to the ticket counter. The sun was coming up, streaking the field with long shadows. I sat there for some time, resting my head in my hands, feeling the bandages at the back of my head, then I got up and walked around the inside of the waiting room, looking at the posters tacked up to the walls, and then went outside again and walked back toward the plane. Oil dripped slowly from one of the propellers, the sun shining on it. It was warm in the sun.

I walked out farther onto the runway. A lone bird, terribly small against the blue sky, circled overhead as though it were a plane about to land, and then flew off toward the east and over the telegraph poles that ran along the road a mile or so away. I seemed to be alone in the middle of nowhere, walking into the fragile silence of the new morning. I continued out to the end of the runway and then turned and walked back to the terminal again.

A young man in a white shirt and wearing a tie was unlocking cabinets behind the ticket counter. He looked up at me as I entered.

134

*"Buenos días, Señor,"* he said.

*"Buenos días,"* I said, and then said in English, pointing to the plane at the edge of the field, "Does that plane go to Mexico City?"

He looked at me and smiled, stopping his work, and I repeated what I had said.

*"Sí, Señor,"* he said, but I knew he did not know what I had asked.

I sat down on the wooden bench and took the ticket out of the book. No one had asked to see it. Then I looked up and saw the young man walking toward me, his heels clicking on the concrete floor. He held out his hand for the ticket and I gave it to him. He looked at it for a moment and then sat down next to me on the bench. I could smell the sweet odor of his shaving lotion. He pointed to the ticket and to a column which said *hora,* underneath which were the figures 0800.

"Thank you," I said, nodding my head that I understood.

He smiled again and got up and went back to his work. Several times after that he left the counter to go into a back room, bringing suitcases and cardboard boxes out with him which he put on the floor next to the counter. The clock above the counter read 6:20.

I turned my head and looked out the window toward the plane. A red fuel truck was driving up to it. A car came toward the terminal along the road. The sun was bright.

The young man at the desk called out to me. I turned back to him and he was motioning me to come to the counter. I walked up to him and saw he had poured two cups of black coffee from a thermos bottle. He gave one to me, and then raised his own and smiled again.

"*Cuidad de México,*" he said.

"*Sí,*" I said.

The coffee was hot and sweet and felt good to swallow. I took the paper cup and went back to the bench. I could hear voices now from the room behind the counter and, from somewhere, the faint sound of music.

# 26

IT WAS TEN O'CLOCK AND THERE WERE many people now in the waiting room. Several announcements had been made by the young man in the white shirt which I could not understand but which I knew were about the delay. I looked again at my ticket and the figures 0800. At 10:15 the young man made another announcement and everyone in the waiting room got up and went out toward the plane. I followed them, waiting around the ladder in the hot sun, and then climbed up to the airless cabin. It was still an hour before the engines started or the plane moved from where it had stopped the night before.

The plane was full, and after we were all in our seats they brought the baggage—boxes and suitcases and crates of one thing or another, and these were first put into a compartment underneath the plane, and then when the compartment was full into the cabin itself at the back of the plane and against the toilet door so that the toilet could not be used.

The people in the plane were quiet, waiting in the heat. Men had their jackets off, the backs of their shirts wet. Several of them had gotten up and were standing in the aisle talking softly to one another. Women sat nervously fanning themselves with magazines, dark stains under their arms. A few children stood up on seats or walked up and down the aisle which was crowded now with the small bags people had brought with them, and with the men who stood there to escape the heat of the cloth-covered seats.

I felt uneasy, the taste of the black coffee I had had earlier still in my mouth. Outside, the sky was white, waves of heat vapor rose up from the concrete, rippling the horizon as though it were water. A pale, nervous man sat next to me, crossing and recrossing his thin white hands in his lap.

Two men dressed in black with gold bands on their sleeves came on board talking rapidly to one another. They worked their way up the crowded aisle toward the forward cabin. In a few minutes the engines started and we taxied out to the runway, the plane like an oven baking in the sun.

I closed my eyes and thought of Mexico City, now only a few hours away. It was too late to go back, even if there had been some place to go back to, it was too late now. But it would be cooler there, because of the mountains.

138

The plane began its attempt down the long runway, shaking more violently than it had before to get into the air. Once it seemed to leave the ground only to return to it with a thud that shook the whole plane. The man who sat next to me had his eyes closed, pressing himself back into the seat. Thin lines of perspiration ran down the sides of his narrow face. He exhaled loudly when the plane finally became airborne, looking past me out of the window and shaking his head with a worried look. He said something to me and I told him I did not speak Spanish. Then he sat back into his seat again and closed his eyes, the perspiration still running down his face, his arms crossed in front of him. He wore a watch on one wrist with a large gold dial that completely covered the thin wrist.

I closed my eyes. The hard paper cover of the note-book had begun to shred in my hands because of the heat and of the wetness of my palms.


The blood had been drained though the carcass still hung from the branch for part of the second day, turning slowly in the wind. For a long time I sat on the front porch looking at it, and at night I dreamed about it, seeing it hanging from the tree and thinking it was still alive. Then Uncle Ben cut it down and skinned it on the lawn in front of the cold cellar. He said that venison was good meat and that I would like it. He had two wash tubs and he put the entrails into one of them. He worked quickly and stopped only twice to sharpen his knife. He separated the deer at the joints and then cut all the meat away from one thin back leg and from a side. He threw the meat into the other tub and told me to carry it into the house. The rest of the meat he said he had to give away because it wouldn't keep and he only liked it when it was fresh. The Overtons from the next farm would appreciate it for they had little money. Though I didn't know that.

I didn't eat supper that night. I went for a walk and sat down by the fence behind the chicken house and watched the sun go down behind the dark shadow of the woods. I kept seeing the deer hanging from the tree, and Uncle Ben cutting into its deep red flesh in the shade of the tree in front of the cold cellar. Father was gone that summer. I did not know where.

Then the sun went down and I couldn't remember for the darkness which came between me and everything else. No one came for me. I stayed there for a long time until the stars came out. I could still see the woods, the dark shadow on the dark horizon. It seemed closer now than when it had been light. I thought of what it must be like to look at a deer down the barrel of a gun and then to pull the trigger, slowly closing your hand around the gun so that the pressure of your finger would be applied evenly and not pull the gun either to the left or to the right but steadily so that the gun would fire straight and the deer would be killed with just that one shot. And if you were hungry and you needed food not only for yourself but for others who were hungry then it would be all right because hunger did not wait but came when it came and there was nothing you could do about it but buy food or steal it if you didn't have money or kill if killing was all there was to do.

I opened my eyes at the sound of the man's voice who sat next to me. He was asleep and he was talking quietly in his sleep and his face was still wet with perspiration even though it had become cooler now in the plane. His face was colorless and he looked as though he was going to be sick. I reached into the cloth pocket on the back of the seat in front of me and found a wax-covered paper bag and opened it and put it on his lap. Then I turned and looked out the window.

The earth was brown with little patches of pale green crisscrossed by narrow lines that I knew were roads. The land was hilly now and I saw the mountains ahead of us.

I would find a place to live. It wouldn't matter where, what it was like. I would find a room somewhere and then I would look for McAllester, and I would try not to think of what had been but only of what would come, and of how I would get through until the next day.

## 27

THE MOUNTAINS WERE BROWN AND there were valleys where the brown of the mountains became green. In the valleys there were villages and lakes and the villages had thin dark lines that ran out of them and then up to the mountains. The lakes were a deep blue and on one of them a small boat with the sun on its white sail glided across the lake and then turned with the wind along the shore. But mostly the land was brown and the mountains looked like crumpled pieces of wrapping paper thrown over the floor of the earth. We were alone with the clouds in the sky and like the boat on the lake the sun was bright on the silver wings of the plane.

The man next to me made a sound and then leaned

forward and put his face between his knees and threw up into the paper bag. He kept his head down and vomited again and again, his dark hair hanging down over his pale face. I turned back to the window. I could see the outlines of Mexico City in the distance. The plane had started its descent.

*This is all there is, there isn't any more.* It was a post card, with only a few words written on it, and it was signed "Love, Dad," and I could read those words because I had often seen them though I could not read the rest of the card because I could not read script then. The card was from another city and when it came Mother showed it to my sister and me and then laid it on the table and said we should begin packing our things.

And so we did, to protect what we had from being broken, carefully putting everything into the boxes which were kept, unfolded and flattened, under the bed at the back of the trailer.

Then we waited for days to hear from him again, and I walked all around the park looking at things I had known since the end of that summer, wondering why nothing was able to remain in any one place for very long. It was fall then and the park was nearly deserted and the air was cold.

But still nothing came, and for days we waited in the cold silence of our thoughts, saying little to one another, while we waited for something to happen. A few things were taken out of the boxes again and one day Mother said Ann and I should go back to school, but then, remembering the note Ann had brought home about our not having lunches in school she said that we had better stay home because it would only be a little while longer and Father would be back and then we would all leave together.

Christmas was coming and we sat down one morning and Mother said we should make Christmas cards and that if we did we could sell them. And Ann thought that was a very good idea and I didn't say anything because I couldn't draw and my handwriting was very poor and there were still letters I couldn't make without having to think of them for a long time and then when I did make them they were always too large and didn't look as though they belonged where I had put them. But we were going to make cards and I could fold the paper in half and then in half again and Mother would write Merry Christmas on the inside and Ann would draw a Santa Claus or a Christmas tree or sometimes just a few snowflakes on the outside.

For two days we worked very hard at making the cards and I folded each sheet of paper carefully so that the corners always came together and there were ninety-one cards when we came to the last of the paper.

Then Ann and I went out to sell them that afternoon and we had all agreed that we would ask three cents apiece for them or two cards for a nickel. We tried first selling them in the trailer park and when we couldn't find many people home we went out of the park and away from the highway to where people lived in houses. But no one wanted to buy the cards and several people asked why we didn't have any envelopes to go with the cards and we said we hadn't thought of it. One woman said if we could come back with an envelope to fit the cards she would be glad to buy one of them and then she asked why we weren't in school and Ann told her it was because we were on vacation.

It was nearly dark when we returned to the trailer. Mother was gone and we were hungry and Ann fried some potatoes and onions and it took a long time for them to cook. While we waited for the potatoes to cook I found some brown wrapping paper folded on the shelf in the closet at the back of the trailer and I took it out and said we could make envelopes out of it. We made three envelopes but they didn't look very good because the wrapping paper had been creased many times and the envelopes looked old and dirty and they spoiled the clean white cards with their Christmas trees and snow-flakes inside. I got mad at everything then because I was hungry and because no one had wanted to buy the cards and I tore up the wrapping paper and threw it on the floor just as Mother came back.

She was angry at first because we had been gone so long and she had been out looking for us, but then she said she was glad we were home and she opened a can of soup neither Ann nor I had seen when we had looked in the cabinets and she poured it over the potatoes and onions. We ate a very good dinner that night and Mother packed the cards away into one of the boxes.

The man next to me sat up and brushed his hair back with one hand and leaned back against the seat though he still held the paper bag between his legs. His eyes were closed and his face was very pale.

The plane banked sharply to the left, one wing dipping down, and I could see the city and it was green and very large. The plane circled several times passing over the city and then over the mountains beyond and I could hear the passengers now as they looked out the windows and talked to each other. It would be more difficult to leave this time because of the distance I had come. And I wondered why I thought again of leaving when I hadn't yet arrived. Motion, the moving through space from one point to another, there was peace in that.

28

THE PLANE LANDED, HITTING THE
runway hard. The man next to me put out one hand to
brace himself on the seat in front of him and he kept
his hand there until the plane came to a stop. We
taxied along another runway and then up to a large
building with a tower built over it. A man in a red
jacket, his hands raised over his head, guided the plane to
a space between two other planes. Then the engines
were cut and everyone got up and took their bags and
slowly filed out, stepping over the confusion of boxes
and crates piled in the end of the aisle, a few of which
had toppled over during the landing. The man who had
vomited had left the paper bag he had used under his
seat and now he stood in front of me holding a brief-

147

case clutched under his arm. He still perspired, though it was cool in the plane, and cool when we stepped down from the ladder, the wind blowing his dark hair. Then he was sick again, leaning against the bottom of the ladder, though no one paid any attention to him. I walked with the others into the building.

I did not know which way to go. I had followed the other passengers in through a gate and then down a long corridor which came out to a large waiting area. I had never seen a building as large. One wall was entirely of glass, and facing it ran a long counter in front of which were several hundred people standing in line, or in groups, or sitting on chairs of bright colored plastic. A voice over a loudspeaker announced the arrival and departure of other planes, in Spanish and then in English, and then in another language I did not know, and then again in Spanish. There was a constant hum of voices, of ringing telephones, and the movement of people coming and going through the building. A dozen or more people pushed past me carrying bags and packages, going into the corridor I had just left. The passengers I had been with in the plane had now disappeared into the crowd milling in front of the long counter or had gone out through the doors in the glass wall through which the sun streamed down like an ocean of light suddenly let loose.

I stood there holding tightly to the book in my hands, people moving around me as though I was an obstacle. I saw a bank of telephone booths between two sets of doors in the glass wall and I went over to it. I looked in the directory in each of the booths for McAllester's name. It wasn't there. The directories were all the same

148

and once I saw that, I carefully looked through one of them, turning the pages slowly, before I gave up. There was no one named McAllester. I picked up the receiver and listened to its silence until a voice came over the line, and then hung it back in its cradle.

I went out of the terminal, passing through the glass doors with other people carrying suitcases, and stood in the warm sun. A blind man with a monkey on his shoulders stood a little ways away, the monkey sitting quietly holding the chain around its neck which then passed to the neck of the blind man.

Several green buses were parked in front of the terminal, and behind them a long row of taxis. I went over to the first bus, which people were entering, and waited. I took out some of McAllester's money and held it in my hand. When I got into the bus I gave the driver a large bill and he took it and gave me a ticket and then other bills. I went farther into the bus and sat down and then carefully counted the bills the driver had given me as change. They were old and dirty and were hard to read. In a few minutes the bus was full and the driver reached out and swung the door shut. The blind man stood in the sun as though waiting for someone, the monkey watching the bus as it pulled away. I had no idea of where we were going except that I felt it would have to be somewhere into the city. I sat back, looking at the shredded cover of the book, and then opened it and read again the few words that were written on the first page, my own handwriting and then McAllester's. I tore the page out, crumpling it slowly in my hand until it was a tight ball.

The bus traveled over broad, smooth highways and

then through narrow dim streets until it came out again onto a wide avenue lined with trees and where tall statues caught the bright light of the afternoon sun. The city seemed made of extremes, of riches and poverty side by side.

The bus stopped around the corner of a side street and before a large glass-fronted hotel. A group of nine or ten people were waiting on the sidewalk, baggage stacked next to them. Everyone in the bus got off. I followed them out and then stood on the sidewalk for a few moments watching the group file into the bus. I had heard some of them speaking English to one another and I thought that maybe I could ask one of them if he knew where I could find a room. But before I could speak to any of them they had entered the bus and the driver looked at me as though he expected me to get back into the bus with them. I turned and walked away.

At the end of the street I crossed the wide avenue which I saw was called the Paseo de la Reforma, and walked past large hotels and movie theaters and restaurants. The avenue was crowded with people and I felt uncomfortable as some of them stared at me. One of the bandages had come loose from the back of my head and was hanging down my neck. I pulled it off and then dropped it as I crossed the avenue again between the rushing cars. There was a small park around a tall monument with a winged figure on top of it, and I sat there for a while away from the crowds on the sidewalk and looked at the city around me. Traffic swirled past the monument, buses and trucks and old cars with the word *Taxi* printed on a sign stuck to the inside of

the windshield. At the end of the avenue there was another monument with the statue of a woman high on
the top of it and with a fountain around a pool at its
base and the water shot up in thin streams into the air,
sparkling in the sun, before falling back to the pool.
Beyond the fountain was a park with two stone lions
at the entrance. I was tired and it seemed hard to draw
my breath. I got up and walked over to the park, going
past the fountain and in between the stone lions and
walking into the park until I could no longer hear the
sounds of the traffic. Then I sat down on the grass,
feeling dizzy and very tired, and again it was hard to
breathe. Then I remembered that the city was over
seven thousand feet above sea level. Driving across the
desert, McAllester had said that, that the city was high in
the mountains. The air was thin and it would be a
while before I would get used to it.

I opened the book again and looked at the blank
page under the cover. Then I realized I still held the
page I had torn out earlier crumpled into a ball in
my left hand. I closed the book and straightened the
crumpled sheet over the cover and then put it back inside the book. Maybe I had not known how to use the
telephone directory. His name could have been there.
There was still time. But what difference would it make?
He had told me to go back. He had given me money so
that I could go back. I was not his responsibility, or
anyone's; it was my life and I would have to manage it.
But perhaps to say thank you, and to tell him that I
would repay the money somehow; because I couldn't
go back to what was never there. I wanted to start all

over again. I wanted to tell him that. I wanted to tell someone that I was going to begin all over again just as though there had never been anything before. But I wouldn't ask for anything. I would do it on my own. I would have to. There wasn't any other way.

## 29

CLOUDS HUNG IN THE SKY LIKE great balloons over the city. I was tired and lay down on the grass, the book under my head. It was cool in the park and a small wind blew at the tops of the trees until they moved back and forth in a slow green dance. A scrap of paper tumbled through the air and then fell to the grass not far away, pausing for a moment as though it could determine its own direction, and then tumbling on again until it was lost in the distance. I felt at peace; as though somehow I would work things out, for existence was all I wanted, being able to go from one day to another. I didn't want more, only a chance to think things out.

Then through the park there came a procession of

stately people marching slowly as though to the beat of a funeral drum, and behind them came women dressed in black, and then a priest in a dark robe who swung silently a brazier by a silver chain, the gray smoke drifting above him and disappearing into the trees. And the women were crying, and the priest was speaking slowly solemn words in a language I had never heard. They passed before me and then young boys in long white shirts carrying plumes of purple cloth which the wind faintly fluttered and then let fall above their heads, and behind them four young men who carried upon their shoulders the statue of a child, and around the statue were hung flowers and then the same purple cloth which fluttered faintly over their faces until only their dark bodies could be seen underneath.

I got up and followed them, looking at the statue and at the way it was held onto the platform the young men carried, how it was held with ropes and wires and a board propped up behind it and how the flowers and the cloth had hidden this from the front. I looked and could see no coffin and I wondered why the women were weeping when there was no coffin.

We came out of the park and into the streets of the city and the streets were narrow and dim with shadows now in the late afternoon. But I soon grew tired of following the procession and stopped in front of an old hotel. A woman stood in the doorway where she had watched the procession as it passed in front of her. She followed me into the hotel and went behind the desk and I asked her for a room and she smiled and shook her head so that I knew she had not understood what I wanted. I pointed to the keys which hung on a board behind her and I took my money and my exit visa out of my pocket and spread them on the desk before her. She took the money and the visa and gave me a key and pointed to the stairs at the end of the hall. I went up the stairs and into the room which opened onto a balcony over the street and from which I could still see the procession though I could no longer hear its voices. In the room there was a bed and a chair and a table with a lamp over it and the room was dark. I turned on the lamp and sat down at the table and opened the book and began to trace invisible words with my finger upon the empty pages while visions guided my hand. And like the women in the funeral procession I began crying and my tears fell on the paper and my finger ran through the drops of water as it raced along the page as though there wouldn't be enough time to put down all that I had to put down to fill the empty pages.

I sat up, feeling the rain on my face. It took several moments to realize that I was still in the park and before I could get up and make a run for the nearest tree. The rain was heavy and I was wet by the time I got to the tree. I saw the book lying on the grass and I went back for it and then ran back to the tree again, wiping the cover of the book as best I could with the inside of my coat. The park was empty and I was wet and shivering from the cold.

But it was more than the cold. I was afraid something again would happen and suddenly I wanted to get out of the park and back to the streets where there were people. But the rain continued and began to drip through the leaves of the tree and I pressed myself up against the trunk holding the book inside my coat and under my arms.

The other bandage on the back of my head had now become loose and I pulled it off and threw it away as I had the first one. I felt the back of my head where the hair had been shaved and could feel the stitches that had closed the two wounds. I would have to find someone to take them out. The hair had already started to grow back. I tried to imagine what I looked like in my wet clothes and with the back of my head shaved and what it would be like if I walked into a hotel and asked for a room. And I thought of Emile then and what it must have been like for him living all those years as he had. But I had not known Emile then. It may have been only the end that was like that. The beginning might have been different.

The rain didn't last long and the sun came out again. In a few minutes the ground was dry as though it hadn't rained though drops still fell from the tree. The sunlight was strong slanting down through the trees and the air smelled clean and I could smell the ground and the rich sweet odor of the earth.

I came out of the park between the two stone lions and stood for a while watching the heavy traffic on the Paseo de la Reforma. There was a tourist bus in front of the park and a man wearing sunglasses handed me a leaflet as I walked past him to a pushcart that was behind the bus. An old man with a short white beard sold pieces of fruit he cut with a long knife on a board that lay across the handles of the cart. I bought a piece of yellow fruit I had never seen before and ate it and it was so good that I went back to the old man and bought another piece. This time he made a great ceremony of cutting open a whole fruit and taking out the large brown seed and giving me the first piece he cut. I stood on the sidewalk eating the fruit and tried to read the leaflet. It seemed to be a schedule of trips out of the city with the times the bus would leave and return. The last trip on the schedule was for somewhere called El Desierto de los Leones and would take three hours. A few people were in the bus, which was large and seemed empty. The man with the sunglasses stood talking to a family of four in front of the bus. The fare was eighteen pesos. I tried to calculate how much that would be in dollars. I knew I had to be careful with the little money I had; I knew it would not go far, as the doctor had said. But the trip would give me time to think and would give my clothes a chance to dry. I brushed my hair back and walked over to where the man stood and waited until the family bought their tickets and then gave the man eighteen pesos. He looked at me and at my wet clothes but didn't say anything. I couldn't see his eyes behind his sunglasses. He was a small man with gold in his teeth and a smile that seemed a permanent part of his face but had no warmth or humor in it. I took the ticket and went into the bus and sat down next to a window. Several times the man climbed into the bus, removing his glasses to count the people in the darkened interior as though he could not remember the number of tickets he had sold. But no one else bought tickets and the man finally came into the bus and started the motor. He did not seem to be happy having to leave with so few people.

The sun was warm through the window, the streets already dry. I was glad I had decided to take the trip, even though I didn't know where it was we were going. But I was used to that, being suspended in space. There would be time to think, to rest.

We drove through the park and then out of the city. I was hungry as the two pieces of fruit were all I had had that day except for a cup of sweet black coffee. I settled back and tried to think of something else, something that I knew was now very important, and then sat up with a start. Coming past us from the opposite direction was McAllester's old Plymouth, the water bag still hung over the front bumper. I turned around in my seat and looked after it as it passed the bus but it was already lost in the traffic.

## 30

L HAD WANTED TO GET OUT AND RUN after him. I got up and went to the back of the bus and looked out the rear window at the traffic behind us. I could no longer see the car; the distance became blurred and indistinct without my glasses. I thought then that I must have been mistaken, that it was too great a coincidence to have seen him like that simply driving down the street; and his name had not been in the telephone directory. I had looked carefully, going over the same page several times, but there had been no one named McAllester.

I sat down again and closed my eyes, remembering the note he had left for me in Hermosillo. What good would it do if I did find him? What would I say to him after I had thanked him for the money? It was my life, not his. Each of us was alone, all of us, always. It was the way things were. No one had anything to do with anyone, except as a witness, someone to watch. And for a moment I thought of my father but could not remember his face, only Emile looking at me from across the fire, and Whitaker's birthmark, and McAllester bending over me with the water bag. But the images were blurred, there was nothing real behind them but only the few moments I had stumbled into their lives taking them with me as I went on again. It was all an accident.

I looked out the window. We had left the city, going down into a valley and then through a squalid village where we stopped for a moment before turning off onto another road. A few people stood watching the bus as it turned the sharp corner, each the same blank face I had seen earlier at the gas station in Santa Ana; and then we climbed back into the mountains again on a dirt road, passing an old man who walked barefoot along the side of the road carrying a dead lamb across his shoulders.

The bus went wildly, careening around curves and alongside cliffs that more than once I thought we would all go over. There were six other passengers, a young man and woman and an older family with two children, a girl and a boy of about eight and ten. They sat in silence, holding on to the seats in front of them, the anger of the driver evident by the way he drove, at having to take the nearly empty bus on so long and un-profitable a journey.

The disappointment was greater when we arrived. A small, mud-colored building sat within a crumbled wall. Tall trees had grown up around everything so that the place seemed even smaller than it was, and dark, forbidding in the shadow of the trees, with the sun going down beyond them, and a chill in the air.

The bus stopped and we remained seated, unaware as yet that this was where we had all purchased tickets to come. The others looked at one another, a whisper of voices passing between them. The driver turned around and said something in Spanish and then got up and left the bus. He leaned against a tree and lit a cigarette, the same cold smile behind his sunglasses which were like two huge green eyes set into his round pockmarked face.

I got up and left the bus ahead of the others. The driver looked at me and pointed to his watch, holding up one finger.

"*Una hora,*" he said.

I nodded my head and went forward, passing through the dark gate and into the yard before the mud and stone walls of the building itself. The others came behind me.

It was dark inside. A placard mounted on a wooden stand just inside the door read in four languages that this was one of the oldest monasteries in the western hemisphere, having been built by monks in the sixteenth century. The Desert of the Lions, though why it was called that it did not say. Life was hard for the monks, there were not many who lived more than a few years once they entered. They never spoke, lived only in silence. A cemetery was beyond the wall.

The others had now come in behind me, standing in the doorway while their eyes became adjusted to the darkness within. The young man and woman, now rid of their fears from the journey, laughed to one another and spoke in a language which sounded like Spanish but which was not, I thought, Mexican. The others, silent but for one or two words which passed like a rope between them, spoke what I thought was German, though it was hard to be sure.

I went through the building, looking at the few crude furnishings of the chapel. Nearly everything was of stone, carved carefully by hand, the marks of the chisel still seen in the stone. At the farthest end of the building, and sunk deep beneath the level of the rock floor, was a cavity hewn from the rock itself which had once been fed by a spring to form a pool. The spring had ceased long ago and the cavity was now only a deep pit in the rock floor. It was cold and damp in the monastery and I wondered what it must have been like bathing in the cold mountain water of the pool and then coming out into the damp air of the dark stone building to be warmed only by the fire of the belief which burned within them, the faith which made everything possible.

I went out into the half-light of the garden, the same crumbling wall enclosing it and running down to where it closed around another building the size of a small cottage. The garden was dead. Even the weeds seemed to have found life too difficult. The stone walks, those separating the brown rocky plots in which something was once grown, were worn smooth, though few had walked on them for hundreds of years. Wars and pestilence and life itself had kept them free of too many feet, but the rain had always come, and the hot sun, the animals scurrying back and forth keeping away from the lions, the soft padded paws of animals. I closed my eyes and for a moment could see the dark space within the broken walls now filled by the monks working the little fields, the silence of the labor, and then they were gone, and I could hear the soft whispering of feet running along the stones, the padded feet of animals running back and forth, the lions waiting forever in the darkness.

The others had gone on ahead to the smaller building at the far side of the garden. I followed them, hearing their voices echo beyond. Small windows dimly lit the interior, the dirt floor hard as the stones of the garden.

At the far corner a narrow doorway led to stairs carved into the rock, and down the stairs were the cells in which the monks had lived, small cramped rooms not large enough to stand in, with only a niche carved into the rock wall for a bed. An electric light cord had been strung along the side of one wall and opposite the entrance to each of the cells, three bright circles of naked light that only increased the darkness of the dozen cells beyond them. The cells seemed like coffins in which the monks slept and woke and prayed and died in the cold damp ground, hearing the lions walk overhead.

The family walked past me and back up the narrow stairs, their children going first, not saying a word. I walked further down the corridor hearing the voices of the young couple. I looked into the cells, each of them the same, barely six feet long and four feet wide, the narrow bed cut into the wall next to the open doorway. I stopped at the last cell at the end of the corridor. The young couple stood against the wall, the man leaning against the woman, their arms about each other.

I turned and walked away, conscious of the sound of their bodies in the cell.

## 31

THE GARDEN WAS DARK WHEN I CAME
out. A greater darkness had fallen in the depth of the
forest beyond the low wall. It was quiet except for a
light wind, the sky still faint with color, a soft pale blue
stretched tightly over the tops of the pointed trees. The
family had gone ahead into the main building, leaving
me alone in the quiet darkness of the ancient garden.

I wanted to write something in the book but I had
nothing to write with; I tried to remember the words
going through my mind, saying them over and over
again so they wouldn't be forgotten. But there were too
many words, too many images crowded upon one another, and there was no way to begin to remember the
words so that I could then be rid of them. For I didn't
want to remember but only to forget, to write them down

in the book and then bury the book somewhere where it would never be found, where it would rot in silence, knowing it was all there and I wouldn't have to carry it with me any more. And perhaps if I could do that I would be free from the past and could go on again only this time alone, beginning all over again as though nothing had gone before, being born out of myself.

I stood in the shadows of where the monks had worked, the book, its cover now ragged, in my hand, and thought of the future, of tomorrow, of years from that moment, trying to imagine how the garden would change, how its desolation would increase. Nothing coming out of nothing, everything moving further and further away from the center, moving into a greater darkness. I wished I had their faith, inured to fear, working silently with my hands until there was nothing but to lie down in the dark cells, bringing the tomorrow of my life one day closer to its last death.

I wanted to lie down. I was tired and there was a dull ache in my stomach from not having enough to eat. I moved slowly through the garden along the wall, broken and open in several places to the forest beyond. A movement in the undergrowth on the other side of the wall made me stop. But the sound, like the rushing of wind through the small leaves, did not come again. Then I went closer to the wall and heard it once more, something that seemed to move in the bushes a few feet away. I closed my eyes and waited, thinking of the monks in the garden behind me, hearing the sound again just beyond the wall, like an animal waiting among the trees.

The fear was always there, the knowledge that nothing would ever change; no matter how many books were buried deep in the earth, they would bring forth their own again, and again and again until the seed was spent, until nothing was left. Nothing coming out of nothing more terrible than whatever had gone before.

The driver sounded the horn of the bus, breaking the stillness of the garden into the sounds of my own breathing, of the leaves weaving among themselves. I opened my eyes to the darkness and saw something, and stared at it until the horn sounded again, and then I quickly turned and went back over the worn stones and into the main building and out again to the gate. The others were all in the bus, though in the garden I had not heard the young couple walk past me. The driver had started the engine and he yelled at me as I came through the gate. I had kept them waiting and they looked at me as I entered the bus. The driver started the bus moving before I had regained my seat so that I was thrown against the seat, the book falling out of my hands and onto the floor between the seats. I sat down and picked up the book, holding it as though it had been injured, and looked back at the dark shape of the monastery now hidden under the trees around it.

This was the way it was, the way it had always been, the way it would be. It was what I had seen beyond the broken wall of the garden, waiting in the depth of the forest beyond the dark silence of the trees. It had been a mistake, from the very beginning it had been a mistake, even from the time before.

The bus went down the mountain road in great leaps,

braking for the sharp curves in the road and then surging on again into the night which was now complete, the trees no longer pointed against the sky, the roots of the dark sunk deep into the earth.

The village was empty when we made the turn through it, a few lights burning in the open windows, but I could see no one either on the dirt streets or in the houses. I breathed deeply, trying to relax, thinking of what I would have to do. My clothes now had dried.


We returned from where we had started, the traffic heavy again around the park, lights dazzling the thin columns of water that shot up from around the fountain by the entrance to the park.

I left the bus and walked up the broad treelined avenue that was crowded now in the evening. I felt uncomfortable among so many people and turned off to the left away from the traffic and from the crowds by the theaters and restaurants. At a street corner stood a small knot of people watching something at their feet, and as I walked past I saw the old blind man again, his monkey dancing a listless dance on the sidewalk while he played a tune on a harmonica, his hat upturned on the pavement before him.

A few blocks farther and the city changed from the bright lights and crowds of where I had left the bus to where it was dark and with only a few people on the streets. Lights hung suspended along the street, breaking the darkness into irregular shapes. I walked for a long time until I could feel the stiffness return to my left ankle again. I came to a small square with a few stone benches inside its iron railing. Around the square there were several cafes, their lights extending out into the shadow of the square. Music and then voices came from the cafes and I stopped and looked into the cafes, listening to the music, watching the people inside eating. I felt in my pocket for the money I had left and then sat down in the square. A few people sat there talking but they paid no attention to me. I took the money out of my pocket and tried to count it, staring at the dirty bills in the light-spill from the cafes. There would be enough for a few days, perhaps even a week if I was careful, perhaps even longer if I were to divide it out to fit a number of days more.

Two men walked past me and left the square going across the street and into one of the cafes. I put the money back into my pocket and looked after them. There was a hotel next to the cafe the men had entered, dark but for one light at the end of the hall, the faded hotel sign lit only by the lights of the cafe next to it. I waited for a few minutes and then got up, brushing my hair back and tucking my shirt into my pants. The thought of being able to lie down, to close my eyes, to sleep in a bed again, made me aware of how tired I was, of how my head had begun to hurt again. I walked across the street, through the bright light in front of the cafe and into the dim hallway of the hotel.

As I entered, a man came in behind me, holding a white cloth in his hand and wiping his mouth with it. He was middle-aged and small and almost like a boy but for his graying hair. He called out to me as he entered and I watched him, waiting until he was closer.

"Do you speak English," I said.

"Sure I speak English; you want somebody?" he said, his mouth still full of food.

"I want a room," I said.

He looked at me and then around me in the half-lit hallway, then behind him as though he expected someone else to be with me.

"I'm alone," I said. "I need a place to stay."

He looked at me and started to laugh, but softly as though he didn't yet understand. I reached into my pocket and took out some of the money but kept it hidden in my hand.

"These rooms are for one, two hours," he said. "You understand?"

"I don't care. I need a place to sleep," I said.

"Nobody with you?"

"No," I said.

He looked at me and smiled, making a gesture with his hands, the white cloth fluttering between us. "You want a girl, is that it?"

"No, I just need a place to stay."

He wiped his mouth again, swallowing.

"Look," he said. "I think you make a mistake, eh?"

I showed him the bills I held. "How much for tonight, just tonight," I said.

He looked at the money and then at me. Then with a shrug he walked by me and took a key from behind a closet door under the stairs. He looked at the key and then at me.

"Twenty-five pesos," he said, and he smiled the same

cold smile of the bus driver. "But you go in the morning, eh?"

"Yes," I said. "I'll go in the morning."

He gave me the key and took the money, not bothering to count it.

"Which room?" I said.

"End of the hall, upstairs," he said. He turned away and started to walk back toward the street. Then he turned his head and said over his shoulder, "But you better knock first."

I went up the dark stairs, hearing his soft laughter as he went out.

# 32

I WALKED UP THE STAIRS AND THROUGH a curtain of black wooden beads that hung from the ceiling at the head of the stairs. The hallway was lit by a single red bulb, the uncertain light gathered around it like moths dancing around a dying flame. I stood waiting for my eyes to become accustomed to the faint light, the beads rattling together behind me like dry summer reeds; and then I began to walk slowly past the shadows of doorways that lined either side of the narrow hall, counting them as I walked, listening for a moment at each one though I heard nothing beyond them but my own movements in the hall. When I came to the end of the hall, a door opened behind me, and turning around I saw a man and a woman come out, the door to their room left open. They went down the hall away from me and then through the beaded curtain, the curtain rattling again in the stillness that was left behind.

I held the key in my hand and looked at the door before me, and then knocked on it softly, the sound muffled by the faintness of my hand. There was no answer. I put the key into the lock and opened the door, letting it swing wide as I stood before the darkened room. I felt for a light switch on the wall to the right but couldn't find one, and then waited for the shadows to settle slowly into shapes I could see.

Thin curtains closed over a window to my right. I walked over to the window and drew the curtains aside and then turned around and looked at the room. There was only a bed, pushed up into a corner, a mirror on the wall next to the bed and running the length of it, and in another corner a toilet bowl without a seat with a washbasin next to it. A bulb hung from the ceiling; a knotted string beneath it hung motionless down to where it coiled on the floor. I went back to the door and closed and then locked it, leaving the key in the lock.

The windows were tall and opened out to a small balcony. I stepped out onto the balcony and heard beneath me the sounds from the kitchen of the cafe next door. The sky was clear, stars filling the night, the wind cool. I breathed deeply, watching the stars, and then shut my eyes, remembering the pool long ago, the lights flickering on the rippling water. For a long time I just stood there, holding on to the cold railing of the balcony, leaning against it, the book under my arm.

Later, I went over to the bed and sat down, kicking off the stolen shoes, hearing them fall softly to the floor. There were no sheets on the bed, only a thin spread thrown over the mattress and pillow. I crawled up onto the bed and lay down. Then I leaned up on one elbow and opened the book. The first page was missing. I stared at the blank white page before me, a small rectangle of pale light on the bed.

I couldn't remember what had happened to the first page, where I had lost it, the page on which I had written the few words about Emile, and McAllester had written that I should go back. But back to where? He couldn't know, and perhaps no one could know, for it was impossible to tell others, words simply said or written down were only words, nothing more. But somewhere it would have to begin.

There was a heavy thudding on the stairs and I sat up, staring at the door as though it would open, and then the sound of the beaded curtain at the end of the hall. A man's voice, and then the light laughter of a woman, voices in the language I did not know, came down the hall. A door opened and then closed, the sounds quieting behind it, and then ceasing altogether.

It would have to begin somewhere, just as it would have to end, the great middle distance, stretching between the two points of beginning and end. Life the beginning of death, the time it takes to die, a little now, a little later. I was tired and wanted to sleep. I forgot about being hungry. I was too tired to want to find something to eat, to have to leave again, to walk back out to the street. I was too tired for that now.

I wanted to sleep. In the morning it would start all over again. I would find something then. There would be time.

I put my hand to the cool mirror, seeing the outline of my body on the bed, my hand touching the mirror, the cool shadow of myself. It seemed strange for a mirror to be next to the bed like that, puzzling; but then I began to understand why it was there.

A cool wind entered the room, the thin curtains by the window billowing out like great waves come in from the night. . . .

Somehow I had always known it would be like this even when I was little and used to sit for hours by myself in the car waiting for everyone to get into it because it was where we all belonged as I did in the back seat where I would sit for hours at a time waiting until someone would come out for me and bring me in for supper and then everyone laughing about how I sat in the car all the time but it was good because it was a safe place for me and they would always know where I was they used to laugh at my waiting there for them and couldn't understand that I was waiting for them to come out so we could move on again hitching the red trailer behind us they thought it strange in a funny way that I should do that as though they couldn't know what I knew that it was always to be like this and going from one place to another was peaceful and I was never afraid like the fear I felt whenever we had to stop for days or for months at a time it was only a pause in a

longer journey that I was afraid of because I knew
something none of them knew but could never tell
anyone the words that I didn't know because I was too
young then to understand all the things that had happened and yet knew what they were or what they had
done to us that made us different from other people
so that we were always strangers who lived somehow in
motion like the waves forever moving along the shore
that never stopped but flowed back and forth forever
and forever coming in and going out so there was
nothing but the movement of the water which I knew
was what it meant and it had always been that way
and it would always be that way because that was all
there was growing in my body until words were there
that I could understand had made no difference like
the years that had passed had made no difference and
one death after another of all the things I thought would
somehow make a difference came and there was no
difference at all but definitions were attached to what
had not had words before and were now only greater
abstractions making everything more difficult to understand they didn't mean anything but were just there
to be one more thing to have to stumble over I didn't
want to think of them anymore and used to sit for
hours at a time watching the waves move back and
forth along the beach of first one ocean then another as
though if I watched them long enough I would understand what it meant to try to reach the shore as the
waves forever tried to do but were each time pulled
back to the mystery of the water lying deep behind them
they could only make their senseless reachings each

176

time failing to do more than touch what they had tried to hold to reach out again like one day following another in the time of our lives that were like the waves falling back to the darkness of sleep until another day came and another attempt was made to hold on to something so that the motion could be stilled long enough to stop the sickness I felt inside of me I wanted to sleep without waking thinking that if this was death then I didn't care anymore because there had been too many deaths and after the first death nothing else mattered except to be as a witness to the coming and the going of the days that were rolled before eternity held back briefly by words which were meant to explain what no one could explain because it was how everything was and love which was meant to ease the pain of life was only like the rock around which the water flowed and which would eventually be worn down by the endless attempts to go beyond it until we came again to the beginning which would be the end of the love which was life and the endless rolling of the waves of our days like our breath upon the water to be stilled by our sleep. . . .

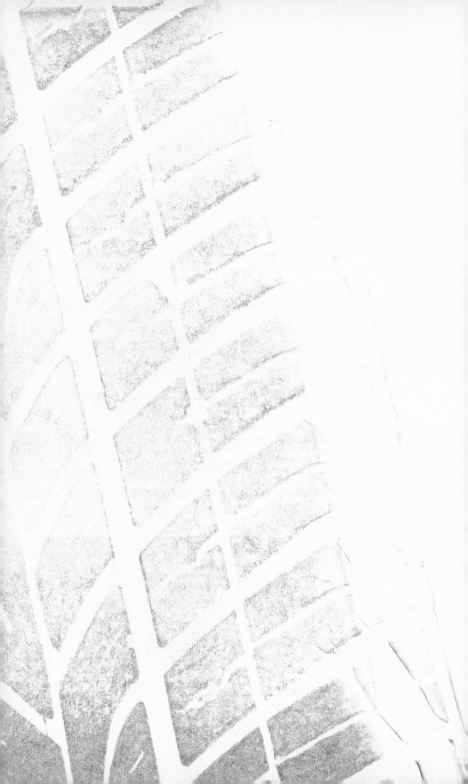